Acclaim for Anjali Banerjee and

Imaginary Men

"The author's hip-hot style combines breezy storytelling [and] wry humor. . . . An engagingly hip debut."
—*The Seattle Times*

"Fresh and highly entertaining. I loved every word."
—Susan Elizabeth Phillips,
New York Times bestselling author

"A *Bridget Jones' Diary* meets *Monsoon Wedding*–style escapade. . . . A fun debut."
—*Publishers Weekly*

"A pitch-perfect romantic comedy . . . reminds us all that the 'lit' in chick lit comes from literature."
—Tara McCarthy, author of *Love Will Tear Us Apart*

"A great read . . . carefree and clever."
—*East West Woman* magazine

"Chick-lit meets Bollywood in this charming novel. . . . Filled with vivid descriptions of Indian customs that will enchant readers."
—*Booklist*

Also by Anjali Banerjee

Imaginary Men

Invisible
Lives

ANJALI BANERJEE

New York   London   Toronto   Sydney

An *Original* Publication of POCKET BOOKS

DOWNTOWN PRESS, published by Pocket Books
1230 Avenue of the Americas
New York, NY 10020

Library of Congress Cataloging-in-Publication Data is available.

ISBN-13: 978-1-4165-1705-4
ISBN-10:   1-4165-1705-7

This Downtown Press trade paperback edition September 2006

10 9 8 7 6 5 4 3 2 1

DOWNTOWN PRESS and colophon are
trademarks of Simon & Schuster, Inc.

Manufactured in the United States of America

For information regarding special discounts for bulk purchases,
please contact Simon & Schuster Special Sales at 1-800-456-6798
or business@simonandschuster.com.

Invisible
Lives

Prologue

The Hindu goddess Lakshmi visited me in my mother's womb. Ma had taken to prowling Kolkata bazaars in a pregnant frenzy, devouring brinjals from street vendors and buying whole inventories of brocade saris. I was constantly jostled about, suffering from motion sickness.

Then Lakshmi floated down on a lotus leaf, her round, kind face a beacon of steadiness. Gold coins cascaded from her four hands, and a red silk sari swirled around her in a current of sandalwood perfume.

"Your parents will name you Lakshmi, my child." Her voice flowed like a Himalayan mountain stream. "People boldly name their offspring after the gods and goddesses, never caring whether the child actually *resembles* the deity."

Since I usually heard only the rush of amniotic fluid, I had no knowledge of my parents' plans.

"In your case, the resemblance will be striking." Her body swelled, fecund and otherworldly.

"Yikes, I'm going to look like that?" I thought.

"But don't go flaunting your beauty. No fashion shows or Bollywood-ing about."

I had no intention of Bollywood-ing anywhere. I just wanted to get out and start living.

"You'll have my gorgeous black hair." She ran her fingers through her shiny tresses, endless and glistening like the Indian Ocean. "Keep it clean. Well washed and brushed. Use only cruelty-free, organic shampoo."

I didn't yet have any hair.

"You're good-hearted, my child." The sari shimmered around her. "You already have the *knowing*, the empathy, the sixth sense. You will discern the longings of others, and you will help them with the textures of silk and vibrant cotton. You will clothe them in hope, Lakshmi, but you will be tested."

"Tested. How?"

"By love, my child. For you, true love will be a long and difficult journey."

"Where will I go?"

"I can't tell you that, can I? I'd be giving away the story of your life." Lakshmi shimmered, burst into a million tiny sparkles, and disappeared.

One

Ma wants me to marry a young Indian Paul Newman, have five male babies, and make a million dollars for our sari shop, all before I turn twenty-eight, which gives me exactly three months.

She doesn't tell me in words, but I sense her old-fashioned longings, as I discern the yearnings of our customers, who pretend to peruse saris while they secretly dream of winning the lottery or the Miss Universe pageant.

I can't say if these dreams will come true. I don't have a crystal ball in my brain. I don't see dead people. The *knowing* is an occasional window into the hidden lives of nervous brides and proud parents, grandmothers, and rebellious teens. They all squeeze into Ma's boutique, Mystic Elegance, which is sandwiched between Northwest Karate and Cedarlake Outdoor Gear. Across from the shimmering lake, the shop is a mini-India just north of Seattle—a soft world of silk and satin. We attract a range of clients, from Americans of all ethnic backgrounds to Indian immigrants who settled here for a variety of reasons—to open businesses or work in the high-tech industry or academia.

Today, while Ma flits around in a turquoise organza sari, I charm a slim, young woman who keeps eyeing the expensive silks. I'm comfortable here, nearly invisible in my glasses, jeans, and baggy kurti blouse, but Ma keeps glancing at me with an anxious look in her eye. She's been on a desperate quest through the Indian matrimonial ads, not for herself but for me. Her yearnings are in overdrive, as if she's holding a delicious secret.

I focus on the slim woman, who is wrapped in a traditional cotton sari, the embroidered endpiece, or pallu, drawn over her head. She holds a paper cup of Seattle's Best coffee, and her woolen coat is damp from the autumn rain.

"I've heard of you, Ms. Lakshmi," she says softly, her voice touched with a lilting accent. "I'm Rina. You must help—I need a long sari that won't slip. It must stay on and cover everything." Her voice teeters along the edge of a cliff. A tiny diamond stud glitters like a lonely star on her nose.

"Why do you want to cover up?" I ask. "You're beautiful."

Pinpoints of color come to Rina's cheeks, and her long

eyelashes flutter. "My mother-in-law's rules," she whispers.

"I see. She lives with you?" Her mother-in-law must come from a traditional community in India. Perhaps Rina is the wife of the second-born son, in which case exposing her head might be considered immodest.

"She arrived from India two weeks back. I've only just come here a year ago to join my husband. I hoped that his mother would not visit. I'm not accustomed to her rules, but what can I say to her? She shouts all the time, insists that I dress formally, even when I'm home. So I put on a sari. But when I go out . . ." She glances down at her clothes, then at my casual getup. A thread of purple longing drifts from her mind. She wants to tear off the sari and pull on jeans like mine and a comfortable kurti over her bra.

I take her hand, and her anxiety hums through me. "Don't be troubled," I say in my best soothing voice. "A sari is simply a length of fabric, pure and unstitched. You can do what you want with it. Remember that."

"My saris have minds of their own, always slipping! I'm constantly worrying that the pallu will fall off my head—"

"I understand. I can help."

Rina's eyes grow bright with tears. "She comes in with tea in the mornings, doesn't even knock! And I must cover up or what a scolding I get—"

"How long is your mother-in-law staying?"

"Only God knows. Perhaps forever."

"Can you talk to her? Explain how you feel? Maybe she'll relax her rules in America."

"I can only hope."

"You'll be fine. I'll show you the perfect sari." I want to rescue Rina. What if her mother-in-law never gives in?

"Thank you, Ms. Lakshmi." Her shoulders relax. "I must confess, I dislike saris. I never wore them much until she arrived. I mean no disrespect, but saris are so difficult to put on—"

"I understand—no need to explain." Rina's worries climb into me. When she ties her sari, how much skin will show? Will the petticoat be too tight? What if the sari falls off altogether?

I know just what to give her.

I search through a sea of saris until I find the perfect raspberry-colored georgette with a floral border. I unfold the sari on the counter. "Very modern," I say. "And this particular sari has a magical quality. It will not slip."

Her eyes light with hope as she runs the semitransparent fabric through her fingers. "It's so thin," she whispers in awe. "So delicate. How—"

"Trust me, Rina. Try it on."

She glances around, as if her mother-in-law might be watching, then scurries into the dressing room. When she emerges, a vision in dark pink, the pallu covers her head as if glued there. "I can't imagine how you found this!" A tear slips down her cheek. "Thank you, Ms. Lakshmi. I'll be back again."

"Take care of yourself." I ring up her purchase at the cash register, and as I watch her leave, warmth settles in my heart. I'm helping women one sari at a time. Soon our shop will expand, maybe even become a franchise, and I'll fulfill Ma's dream and marry the perfect, supportive husband.

And yet I'm restless, as if a jumping bean is leaping around inside me. What if I end up like Rina, a nervous insomniac worrying about exposing too much skin? I'll make sure I marry a man whose traditions match those of my family. But what if I never find him? *Love will be a long journey,* the goddess said.

I have little time to obsess upon such problems, for Mrs. Dasgupta, elderly matriarch extraordinaire, strides in, shaking water from a black umbrella. She flings her silver pallu over her shoulder. She always wears a formal sari to our store. I've never seen her in western clothes.

Surrounded by customers, Ma motions to me to help. I press the palms of my hands together in a gesture of greeting. "Mrs. Dasgupta! I've put aside some lovely silks for you."

"I don't want silk today. Have you cotton?" she shrieks. Her thoughts blow past me like newspaper tumbling along a sidewalk. *Blue cotton sari, sandalwood scented, pale as an anemic sky. A shadow-man smiling in the background.*

I give her my best patient smile. "Our Bengali cottons are mainly white, but let me see what I can find."

"You always give me just the right sari. My friends say, 'Pia Dasgupta drives all this way for a bit of cloth?' But I tell them, Lakshmi Sen knows." She presses a gnarled finger to her forehead. "You always know what it is I am thinking."

"I'm a good guesser." I pull more saris from the shelf. "We have fine handloom cotton. One of a kind, each of them."

Mrs. Dasgupta snorts, fingering the fabric. "Gold border is also handwoven? What is this design?"

"Auspicious—peacocks." I trace the handwoven threads. "These are long saris, won't show your ankles." Mrs. Dasgupta would consider a short sari lower class, hiked up to the knees so women can work in the fields.

"What is it I'm looking for? My nieces arrive from Mumbai tomorrow. We're having a family reunion—"

"You still want cotton? What about festive Madrasi silk?"

"Far too bright. I'll not wear the silly garlands in my hair."

Despite the autumn chill, my armpits break out in a sweat. I pull out sari after sari in different colors and patterns.

Mrs. Dasgupta frowns. "What are you thinking with this red one, that I am just getting married? And this yellow— I'm not rolling around at temple, and I'm not pregnant. Three boys are quite enough, and lucky I am not to have given birth to girls."

"I brought you red and yellow because you look so young and beautiful." I hold her hands, as brittle and parched as fallen leaves. It's a wonder her fingers can support all those ruby-studded rings. An image of forgotten youth breathes through her skin, races up my arm into my brain. She's maybe sixteen again, her hair blue-black, down to her knees. She's wrapped in a crimson wedding sari embedded with jewels and gold. She holds the translucent pallu coyly over her face, giggles at a slick young Indian groom with a bulbous nose. Then the shadow-man appears, her sari changes color to pale blue, and her longing for him hits me like a bowling ball.

I let go of her hand. Such specific images visit me rarely—I've never sensed longing so acute, so raw.

"Well, you think I look young?" Her lined face softens, and she pats the white bun on the back of her head.

"Not a day over twenty-nine," I say.

"And my skin is looking so *fair*, nah? Must be the Light & Lovely cream. Have you got any more?"

I give her a tube from the glass case. In India, fair skin is highly prized. Our customers swear by Light & Lovely. You won't see an Indian in the Mango Bay Tanning Salon on the corner.

Mrs. Dasgupta pops the tube into her massive handbag. "Now I shall look even younger."

"And yet you hold the wisdom of the world." I'm busy

searching for a sari in a crimson print, like her wedding sari.

"You're buttering me up. What about you? Twenty-seven and no sign of marriage. Your ma is quite concerned." The lines deepen around her mouth.

"She needn't worry." I glance at my mother, gliding around in translucent organza. She hides her secrets behind a wide, toothy smile. Golden bubbles of elation bounce around her—bubbles that only I can see. What is she up to?

"Could you not find a good Indian husband when you lived in New York?" Mrs. Dasgupta says. "Your ma says you were there for three years, gallivanting around on Wall Street. There must be rich Bengali bachelors there, nah?"

"I wasn't on Wall Street. I worked at a small investment firm, and I was always busy." I can't tell her about my many disastrous dates with colleagues and high-powered executives, about my fruitless search for the perfect relationship.

Mrs. Dasgupta smacks her lips. "Young women these days, so independent. Career girls, nah? And now you're all the time working for your mother."

"The shop is a full-time job, I must admit." Maybe Mrs. Dasgupta forgot that I own half the store now, that I'm the one keeping the business afloat. Ma might be a whiz at buying fabrics, but she doesn't know a plus sign from a minus, payables from receivables.

"You must look for a groom full-time instead. Your ma has been saving your dowry money since you were *choto*.

This small." Mrs. Dasgupta pats the air two feet above the ground. "Such is the case with girls. Their parents must pay for everything while the husband's family sits back and holds forth. They will want a huge feast, expensive jewels, a thousand wedding guests."

A guest list of a thousand is common for Bengali weddings. But what about a husband? I picture Ma's delighted face at my wedding, a grand Bengali affair to cement the relationship between the two extended families.

Maybe I'll have to go to India to find my match.

"Lakshmi?" Mrs. Dasgupta is tapping my arm. "Are you all right?"

"Sorry, I was just thinking about weddings." The goddess said love would test me, but how will I recognize love? Did I love Rijoy, the eccentric but handsome entomologist I met as an undergrad? He loved the University of Washington and still works there as a research fellow. We had fun, but he was most interested in studying insects. So I escaped to New York after graduating, where I finally met Sean, the suave American financier, fluent in five European languages. Despite my education and upbringing, my skin was still too brown for his blue-blooded family.

He wouldn't introduce me to his parents.

"You're considering only appropriate men from your community, I should hope," Mrs. Dasgupta is saying.

She means my family's community in Kolkata.

"Of course," I lie. She is hopelessly old world. The truth is I have to cast a wider net here. I've dated Americans, Italians, a German exchange student. But I suppose I've always known, deep in my Bengali subconscious, that I would eventually come full circle, home to family and tradition.

"Then you can be certain of the way the boy was brought up," she says. "That he is a good boy of good breeding."

"Of course. But it's difficult here—"

"That's why you must go back to India."

"I go occasionally with Ma on her buying trips—we've been looking everywhere, believe me. She's introduced me to family friends—"

"Then you must look harder or your ma will become old and wrinkled and still her daughter will remain unmarried. And what would your father have thought?"

Don't bring Baba into this, I want to say. But I smile politely and pat Mrs. Dasgupta's arm. "Always watching out for us. How kind you are."

"And why you wear those ugly glasses and tie your hair back, I don't know. Men want a beautiful wife these days, nah? Never mind if she can't cook, clean, take care of the household."

"But I can cook and clean, Mrs. Dasgupta. I don't enjoy Bollywood-ing about."

"Your Ma taught you well, but men these days want a wife they can parade around."

"A good man will see past these glasses." I glance at Ma, who gives me a look pregnant with unspoken secrets, a new idea popping from her sleeves in those bright golden bubbles. Maybe she's found me the Bengali prince of her dreams, like Pooja's fiancé. Dipak is kind, handsome, and smart, and Pooja loves him. She is our slim part-time intern, all frizzy hair and elbows, off helping two teenage girls in the shawl section. In Dipak, she's found herself a perfect match.

Only Mr. Basu, Ma's right-hand man, remains unmarried at fifty. His engagement fell through when his fiancée ran off with a prince, and Mr. Basu never quite recovered. His bald head, round body, and slightly sour odor don't help his prospects much, and neither does his propensity to hide in the back room unpacking boxes.

The golden bubbles burst, and fragments of Ma's jumbled worries break through—she's probably fretting about the leak under the bathroom sink.

Mrs. Dasgupta keeps chattering. "—to see past your specs, a man needs to have X-ray vision like that Superb-Man, or what's it—"

"Superman," I say. "Maybe I *am* waiting for a superhero." I let out a hollow giggle and push the glasses up on my nose. Nobody knows they're plain glass, not prescription lenses. The elastic hair band is so tight that it's yanking the ponytail from my scalp. I can't let my hair down in the shop, where brides-to-be wobble in nervously on cold feet. The goddess told me not to flaunt my beauty.

"—and you've studied the Rabindrasangeet?" Mrs. Dasgupta goes on. "Lovely songs, nah? The perfect expression of Bengali culture."

"I love to play the piano, mainly classical," I tell her. Erudition and musical skills are coveted assets to make a prospective wife more attractive, but to me, music is a blissful escape from the longings of others.

"And the Kama Sutra?" Mrs. Dasgupta gives me a sly look.

"Mrs. Dasgupta! Really!"

She lowers her voice. "I call it Kama Sutra for your benefit, but I know it as Kamasutram, and it is about the *science* of love, not at all about what the Americans think! Only twenty percent is about you-know-what! Written by the great Vatsyayana. He was a celibate scholar, did you know?" She sounds reverent, as if his celibacy somehow made him an expert on sex.

"Fascinating, Mrs. Dasgupta." The blood heats my cheeks. I don't want to imagine her in exuberant youth, practicing all sixty-four positions of the Kama Sutra. With her shadow-man!

She's fingering the saris and thinking of him. Then the image of her husband's bulbous young nose returns, and she's at her wedding again. The ceremonial fire rises in bursts of flame, the crimson wedding sari burning away, leaving only the gold and jewels. She still wears those gems on her fingers, around her neck, in her earrings.

But who was the shadow-man? What about the blue sari? Did she wear it for him?

I know just what to give her!

"How about this new soft cerulean blue muslin?" I unfold the sari on the countertop, and the heady scent of handwoven cotton fills the air. "This wasn't mass produced. A master weaver made this—it's very expensive."

"Oh, *my* goodness." She leans over the counter, and the pallu slips from her shoulder. Her thoughts burst with pulsing hearts of happiness. She flips the sari back over her shoulder. "How did you know about this blue?"

The door swings open, and the whole store goes silent. A damp breeze wafts in on a current of exquisite floral perfume. Even before I glance toward the door, I know someone important has arrived. A faint imprint of thoughts drifts toward me—color and brightness, a swirling burst of rose petals.

Mrs. Dasgupta turns around, and her mouth drops open. "Oh, Shiva," she whispers and elbows me. "Is that who I think it is? Coming into your store? Oh, what I will tell my friends!"

If it weren't for the wall clock ticking away the hour, I would think time had stopped. Customers freeze, holding kameezes or earrings, mouths stop in the open position, words stick to the air. And still the rose petals swirl toward me.

Ma's on the move, hurrying to greet the new customer, a beautiful young woman in a wheelchair, her leg thrust forward in a cast. She's in black slacks, floral silk shirt, and a purple coat beaded with raindrops, the blustery storm rushing in around her. Shiny black hair cascades past her shoulders. Her perfect oval face shines, and her wide, long-lashed eyes exude divine beauty. Only this woman is not a goddess, she's a Bollywood actress, Asha Rao. I recognize her from *Star* magazine.

If I whip off the glasses and let down my hair, I'll look as radiant and beautiful as Asha. And that's precisely why I keep my head down, glasses on, my figure hidden beneath the baggy shirt. The last time I showed my beauty, the customer, a bride-to-be, fled the store in a huff and took her business elsewhere.

"Asha Rao," Mrs. Dasgupta says in a hysterical whisper. "In your store. Ah, Lakshmi. What is happening?" The blue sari slips from her fingers. Time moves again as customers stare at Asha. Their longings crowd in. Some want her to be their daughter, their sister. Some want to be a Bollywood actress like her. Some want to throw her off a cliff and steal her life. Some want to steal her fiancé, the jet-setting hotelier and actor Vijay Bharti—hooked nose, big hair, and all. Asha's thoughts bounce out into the fray. She imagines dancing with Vijay in a Bollywood musical, rose petals fluttering down all around them. An entourage of fans bobs in the background.

I feel him before I see him—a deep, reckless presence, a man who could jump from a plane at high altitude, brazenly sure that his parachute will open. In a tailored black suit, he's pushing Asha in the wheelchair. His blond hair is long, parted on the side, and he's tall, broad-shouldered, large as a quarterback. His eyes are the blue of hard-cut gems.

He steps across the threshold and the door slams, trapping a pocket of the storm inside with us. The rose petals fall away, sucked down an invisible drain into the cosmos. Someone pressed the mute button on everyone's secret thoughts, shut the window, closed the curtains.

I sense no longings, no thoughts, no deep desires from others. I'm blind to it all and gasping for breath, a goldfish flung from its bowl. In the space of a moment, my entire sixth sense collapses and disappears.

Two

I close my eyes and reach for images, but nothing comes except the orange and black Rorschach blots on the backs of my eyelids. I snap my eyes open, squint in the harsh light. The blood drains from my face. I brace my hands on the counter to keep from toppling over. The lights brighten, perfumes assaulting my nose. The rustle of saris turns into grating noise. Is all this happening because the *knowing* escaped into the storm?

"How can we help you, Ms. Rao?" Ma's saying. "We're thrilled to have you in our store."

Mrs. Dasgupta blinks, her mouth slightly open in wonder.

"Vijay and I are eager to marry," Asha says in a well-modulated, stagelike voice. "The auspicious date comes very soon, or so Vijay's astrologers and gurus say! And we haven't time to return to India right away. Later, we'll have three more ceremonies in three Indian cities, but for now, I've got to stay here to make this blasted film, and so—"

"You would like us to help with the wedding here," Ma says.

"We need to clothe all the family and friends," Asha says.

"Of course. We work quickly." Ma breaks into a confident smile, revealing one crooked eyetooth, the rest slightly stained from years of tea. She gestures toward me. "I'm sure you've heard of my daughter's ability to—"

"Choose the right fabrics?" Asha turns and gives me a dazzling smile. "You know the Desi community. Everyone knows everything. Indians here must have each others' houses bugged."

"Then you've come to the right place." Hope and anxiety shine in Ma's eyes, but her thoughts have melted into the Northwest rain. She knows about my heightened intuition, but I've never revealed the true extent of my ability. I don't want to tell her that the *knowing* has suddenly flown the coop.

I can't let her down. Not now.

Mrs. Dasgupta goes pale, clutching the blue sari.

Asha glances around at the staring customers, then lowers her voice. "We need the whole place to ourselves for the time being, nah, Mrs. Sen?"

"Of course, of course." Ma springs into action, ushering people out, apologizing, telling them she'll open early tomorrow, the shop is temporarily closed.

I ring up Mrs. Dasgupta's purchases, and she scuttles out of the store.

I smooth my shirt and take deep breaths, but a touch of nausea climbs through my stomach. Ma's features sharpen. Her gold hoop earrings glitter, and the molecules of powder on her cheeks glint beneath the bright lights.

I stride forward and take Asha's hand. Her fingers are soft and supple, almost limp. "I'm Lakshmi, at your service," I say in a firm voice. "Let me know what you're looking for and I'll be happy to help."

"We carry a variety of styles," Ma says. "Even woven wedding saris from Banaras—"

"Banarasi, the best!" Asha Rao sucks in a breath.

I wonder if she's faking the awestruck act, but her thoughts have slipped into the ether. I'm adrift with no steering.

Ma leans in toward Asha. "Have you heard of sangol paria?" Her eyebrows rise the way they do when she's telling a secret.

Asha shakes her head, motions for the blue-eyed man to wheel her forward to examine the gold jewelry in the glass cases. Why does she need him to push her? I wonder if he's her secret lover. But she's getting married!

Ma runs after them. "Rare, prized saris from Southern Bihar—no two are alike. They become prized family heirlooms."

We don't actually *have* any sangol paria saris. What is she up to? "Ma, I don't think—"

"Intricately woven textiles," she says. "Absolutely unique among Indian saris."

Unique! I try not to roll my eyes.

"Unbelievable," Asha says.

"Virtually unavailable in the cities," Ma goes on. "But still woven in remote areas. Highly coveted."

"Then I'd like to see one. Price is no object." Asha motions to the man, and he wheels her forward. I step out of the way.

Price is no object. Ma must think she's died and gone to the heavens with the triumvirate of Hindu gods, only we don't actually have any sangol paria!

"We have muga silk!" I say, coming to Ma's rescue. "And golden wild silk found only in Assam. You might like them better."

Asha breaks into a movie star grin. "I will see the muga silk. I must give saris to Vijay's sisters and mother and all the aunties. Have you got the staff for such a project?"

"Of course, no problem!" Ma says.

"Are you quite certain?" Asha glances around the boutique. "I see only a couple of clerks." Her lips turn down with disapproval, as if an army should've been waiting for her here. We can't yet afford more staff unless Ma uses my dowry money, which she would do if the temperature in hell dropped below freezing, the sky turned orange, and dinosaurs roamed Seattle.

"We've got a seamstress, a dedicated buyer, and excellent customer service," Ma says.

All rolled into one, I want to say.

"How perfectly lovely then!" Asha says. "We'll sit and talk and plan, nah? Lakshmi, you must come and visit me on the set."

"That will be an honor for her," Ma says. "Lakshmi and I will help you find what you need."

I glance back toward the counter, where Pooja and Mr. Basu stand mesmerized, staring at our Bollywood guest.

"I can't get around much for the next few weeks," Asha is saying. "Broke my leg in a stunt. You might've read about it—I do all my own stunts, you know. You'll have to let Nick be my arms and legs. Oh, by the way, Nick's my driver and sort of my bodyguard." She giggles.

The silent man nods slightly.

Ma gives him a perfunctory look, dismissing him as an invisible servant.

"Pleased to meet you," I say.

"At your service." He shakes my hand, nearly crushing my bones with his grip.

"We need custom-sewn suits for the little nieces," Asha says. "Do you have?"

"We have many shalwar kameezes and many fabrics," Ma says. She takes Asha and her driver all over the store, showing them variety and rarity, and I move as if in a dream until Asha tugs my arm, her face aglow. "We have to run for now, but oh, Lakshmi, you have the most divine designs. All the elements must match. I'll be back tomorrow afternoon!"

Nick wheels her toward the door. As soon as they leave, the *knowing* rushes back into me, as if it's been here all the time, hiding behind the shawls. I exhale with relief, welcoming an old friend. My fingers tremble, and I feel like I've just run a marathon.

My ability waxes and wanes like a temperamental moon, but it has never completely disappeared!

Ma's tugging my sleeve. Her eyes are bright with barely contained excitement. "Isn't it lovely that the gods have brought us Asha Rao?"

Strictly speaking, it was the driver who brought her. "Wonderful, Ma!"

"How could we have such luck? Your sensitivity is a divine gift, as I've always said!"

She doesn't know how right she is.

"Well, my dearest Bibu, this is a day for the history books. And there is something else. I meant to tell you later at home, but I simply can't wait. Besides our new business, it's the most wonderful news in years."

"What is it, Ma?"

She presses her hands to her cheeks, and tears glisten in her eyes. So this is what the golden bubbles were all about, the secret she hid so well. "Oh, Bibu. I have finally, finally found the perfect husband for you."

Three

*M*a's golden bubbles become dandelions that dissipate in the air, replaced by pink rhododendrons. Flowers bloom from her when she's happy. And when Ma's happy, I'm happy. She drags me into the office and collapses into her squeaky chair. "They say good fortune comes in threes, nah? First Asha, and now this. What shall be the third thing?"

"Who is this perfect bachelor, Ma?" I ask as I perch on the desk in front of her.

"My dearest, do you remember the Gangulis?"

"Baba's old friends from Kolkata? Dilip Ganguli went to college with Baba, right?"

"Baba always wanted you to marry well. He adored Dilip and Dilip's only son, Ravi. Do you remember?"

"Baba spoke of him, a long time ago, I think." *Ravi,* a boy mentioned in my father's last letter to me before he died.

"He's only a few years older than you." Ma takes my hands in hers. "Ravi is unmarried, and he's coming to Seattle for a job! He's a doctor. Can you imagine? He wants to meet you. He's very much looking for a wife."

"Ma, you've outdone yourself."

"He's quite handsome, and he is your match in every way. Well-educated, highly cultured, kind, and considerate. He has always taken great care of his family. I've spoken to his ma at length. I've told her you cook well, you've got your degree in business to help with the shop, that you're a good girl, living with your ma, that you are so beautiful and quite bright. I think this is what attracted Ravi, you know." Ma's face is aglow with happiness.

"Ma, you're amazing."

"We must go to India to meet him in three weeks—"

"So soon!"

"I've already got our tickets. Besides, I must go to consult with a distributor for my spring fashion line," Ma says. "What luck! You will meet him, won't you, Bibu?"

"Of course I will." I embrace her in a tight hug. She feels fragile, her bones insubstantial despite the illusion of strength she projects for the customers. The goddess's words return. *Love will be a long journey.* This is it. I must go to India.

"He's going to send you an email with a snap of himself," Ma says. "I've already sent him a snap of you without the glasses, with your hair down. You must put your best foot forward."

"I doubt it's my feet he's interested in, Ma. I'll be beautiful for him." I twist my hands in my lap. She already sent a picture? From my bio-data portfolio? I lean forward and take Ma's hands in mine. Her fingers are warm, the skin slightly rough. Mrs. Dasgupta's voice echoes in my mind. *She has been saving your dowry since you were choto.* "Ma, you need to dip into my dowry money to help with rent, just until the store is on solid ground—"

Ma yanks her hands away and sits square and straight, shoulders back. "I'll not touch your dowry, Bibu. That is your money, for your happiness, for your future. Besides, I carry only the finest fabrics. I am the only one in the Seattle area who imports a variety of saris from the farthest corners of India. My customers know this. I have no shortage of business."

I bite my lip. "But our overhead has skyrocketed. The rent has risen, and—"

"We'll pay. We always pay. This new business will help!"

"But you can't always wait until the fifteenth of the month—"

Her voice softens the way it does when she's angry. "Are you trying to tell me how to run the business, Lakshmi Sen?"

"No, Ma." But I'm taking care of the books, taking care of you, taking care of your happiness. "You've done a lovely job with the store."

She smoothes her sari and runs her fingers across the red stain of vermilion in her hair part. She still wears that stain, indicating her married status, although my father has been dead twenty years. That small gesture, her fingers on that memory in her hair, touches my heart. I wish she could find another man, but she claims not to be lonely. I wish I could see inside her, to the private longings that will not be revealed. The *knowing* does not penetrate the deeper secrets of her heart, where I'm sure my father still lives.

Four

The world is my sari, the sari my world.

I wrap myself in the comfort of fragrant fabric, sur-round myself daily with the variety and subtlety of silk. I see golden brocade borders flapping in the sky, embedded in wisps of cloud. While a stranger might discern only the surface of organza, cotton, or chiffon, I hear the sigh of love, smell the thick smoke in Kolkata streets. I hear the calls of a street vendor, the squeak of a rickshaw.

If you look closely enough at a woven sari border, you'll catch a woman's history. She uses her pallu as a pocket for keys, to shield her face from pollution or from the advances of men. She plays with the fabric to be coy, lets her husband unravel the cloth in the privacy of their bedroom.

Since my earliest days, saris have carried the whispers of my ancestors. I keep a burgundy silk worn by my great-grandmother Kamala, for her arranged marriage to my great-grandfather Mohan. The imprint of his love for Kamala is trapped forever in silk. Kamala found her match and created a great, timeless bond with him.

My mother lives to find me such a match so that she will not have to endure her family's pestering her—*Your daughter is still unmarried, what a burden on you, and you will have no grandchildren.*

I hope that Ravi and I will share a bond, the kind that Pooja shares with Dipak. They've known each other since childhood.

Just before closing, Pooja comes to me with a tight, worried expression on her angular face. "Lakshmi—my parents want me to do a wedding rehearsal next weekend, at the Hindu temple in Bellevue." She sits at my desk and fingers a paper clip.

"Congratulations, Pooja!" I pat her shoulder, and an image expands in my mind—Pooja rushing down a noisy, bright hallway, white coat flapping behind her, stethoscope around her neck. Then the picture whirls down into the paper clip and disappears. My fingers are gripping her shoulder. "Pooja, do your parents know that you want to be a doctor?"

She swivels the chair around and looks at me, her eyes wide. "Pediatrician. I love kids. Did you see it?"

I nod. "They would be very happy."

She drops the paper clip and rubs her nose. "I know—
it's just—I want to go to San Francisco to study, and
Dipak's going to the UW here. I don't know about the
long-distance relationship thing. And my parents want me
close to them. Our wedding wasn't supposed to be so soon!
But apparently the date is in the stars."

"You think your parents won't let you go to San Francisco? I worked in New York, and I came back, and all is
well."

"They would let me go, if they knew. But I love them
and I love Dipak. We were friends first, and that's a good
thing, right?"

"Can you picture yourself married to him?"

Her eyes light with a spot of hope. "Yes—we talked
about it when we were kids. We even pretended to be
married."

"How lovely." A tiny knot twists below my ribs. Am I
jealous? Do I wish I had a fiancé whom I'd known all my
life, of whom I could be certain?

"But you know, Lakshmi, when Asha came in, I took
one look at that driver, and I thought, he's so cute!" She
giggles.

"The chauffeur? Pooja!"

"I guess I got cold feet, wondering what it would be like
to have a totally different life without Dipak. Silly of me."

I take Pooja's hands. "I'll go with you to the rehearsal, how's that?"

She gives me a grateful look. "Would you do that?"

"I'll pick you up at your apartment." Pooja lives on the hill, on the other side of the lake, and rides her bike to work.

"I owe you so much, Lakshmi."

"You owe me nothing. And I want you to tell Dipak about your dream of going to medical school in San Francisco. And your parents. I'm sure you'll work it out."

But Pooja doesn't look so sure.

That evening, Ma and Mr. Basu are still opening new shipments when I take off the glasses, let down my hair, and leave the shop in twilight. I don't worry about Ma walking home alone. If she works past dark, Mr. Basu drives her.

"Hey, Lakshmi!" Chelsea calls from next door. "You're leaving early today. It's only six." She's leaning in the doorway of Cedarlake Outdoor Gear. She's in lime-green jogging pants, a matching long sweater stretched across her ample figure, and she's drinking her usual bottle of iced tea. No matter what the weather, she drinks iced tea and wears Birkenstocks sandals over woolen socks. Her short hair is dyed a pale blond this week. Last week it was red. She's owned Cedarlake for a year, and although she's not much of an outdoor enthusiast, she knows all the gear. Her longings are simple—dinner with a friend, a movie, a visit to her sister's new bungalow. But she harbors a dark worry that I can't yet discern—concern for someone in her family.

"Busy day. I'm beat. How're things for you? Slow this evening?" I stop and peer into her store, which stays open until nine. A few customers mill about in the rain gear section.

"Big bike race in the city today. Everyone must be over there. Who was that in your store? Some kind of celebrity? The whole neighborhood's talking, I swear. She looked familiar, showed up in a limo—"

"Big Bollywood actress. She's making a film here."

"Bollywood? Isn't that like the Indian Hollywood? Don't they make a million musicals a year over there? What's she doing here?"

"Filming her first American movie—"

"In this lousy weather? Those clouds are mocking me. Every time I head out for a walk"—she pats her fleshy hips and glances at the puckering sky—"the rain comes again. They don't call Seattle the rainy city for nothing."

"It's also the Emerald City, Chelsea. A beautiful place for making a film. *Say Anything, An Officer and a Gentleman*—lots of movies were filmed in Seattle. *Get Carter,* with Sylvester Stallone—"

"Yeah, but a Bollywood-type movie? Oh!" She claps a hand over her mouth, and her hazel eyes widen. "Now I know where I saw her. Asha Rao! On TV, *Northwest After-*

noon! She was talking about a new movie being produced by this new indie company, Emerald Films. It's a love story, a drama. An American guy falls for an Indian, or something. . . . It's called *Who's Sari Now?*. Kind of like *Bride and Prejudice.* She was talking about how hard it is to work while wearing a cast. She's filming all the sit-down parts now. When she gets the cast off, she'll do more stunts. Wow! She came into your store. You rock!"

"She's been called the hottest bachelorette in Bollywood, but now she's getting married."

Chelsea swigs the last of her iced tea. "I'd like to get married someday, even have kids."

"No boyfriend in the cards?"

"My only date for the weekend is with my nephew—his birthday party. He's my sister's son." Her lips turn down in a slight frown, and I see her climbing the porch of a modest Craftsman bungalow, a gift box in her hands. Inside, a slim blond woman, probably Chelsea's sister, kneels beside a small boy, who is throwing a tantrum on the hardwood floor. The woman tries to lift him into her arms, but he slaps her away, punches and pummels her, sending her stumbling backward, stunned. Chelsea stands in the open doorway, not moving, barely breathing.

The boy's mother reaches out a trembling hand, palm forward, and finally he presses the palm of his hand to hers. As their fingers touch, I know that this is the closest he will ever let her come. He can't handle spontaneous displays of affection, the usual cuddles and kisses we all take for granted. His mother, and Chelsea, and everyone who loves him, will have to settle for this distance.

His screaming has faded to a whimper.

Chelsea is watching me, pinpoints of pain in her eyes. She doesn't know what I see in her mind, and I don't yet know her well enough to tell her.

"If you ever want to talk about anything, just hang out sometime, I'm game," I say.

She smiles absently. "Sure, we could grab a brew or something."

"I don't drink, but coffee would be okay."

"Chai. Cool."

"We could talk about—your sister." Oh, lame, lame! I admonish myself.

Her eyes narrow. "Lillian? What about her? Do you know her?"

"Lillian, that's a nice name," I say. "I heard something about her. Doesn't she come into your shop occasionally?"

"Sometimes—she talked about checking out your shop sometime, too."

"I'll give her a good deal," I say.

Chelsea nods, gives me a funny look, and disappears into her shop. I let out a long breath. That was a close one—I nearly spilled the beans. If I do, Chelsea might think I'm prying, or worse, she might steer clear of me altogether.

The sidewalk stretches away, voices and laughter coming at me in shards. I am so close to the world, so close to hidden longings, and yet separate, alone.

I stop in at Cedarlake Café for a latte. Heads turn to stare, but I'm used to it.

"So, Lakshmi the beautiful." Marcus winks at me from behind the counter. He's a tanned version of Brad Pitt with a sweep of auburn hair, a goatee, and small silver earrings. "When are you going to go out with me? *The Glass Menagerie* is playing at the Rep downtown."

"And you're not in it? How can that be?" I sidestep his question. He's a handsome artist and actor, but no sparks fly between us. I place a ten-dollar bill on the counter. "My usual soy latte, please."

"I didn't make that play, but I got an audition for *Cat on a Hot Tin Roof*." He bites his lip, and I see him in a white spotlight onstage, reading from a script. His voice wobbles, but soon he relaxes and falls headlong into the role.

"You'll do great," I tell him. "This may be your big break."

"You think?" His eyes twinkle with excitement.

"I have a good feeling—kind of like a sixth sense."

He adds an extra shot to my latte. "No charge."

I leave the café feeling light on my feet. My day can yield diamond moments like these, and as I pop open my umbrella against the mist, I wonder where else I would be if not here, helping people in small ways in the shop. Perhaps I would've made principal at Overseas Investments. I was good at crunching numbers, good at peering into the complex minds of my colleagues. I could climb the corporate ladder with ease, like an acrobat in a circus, never having to look down.

But New York proved too frenetic for the *knowing*. And then Sean and I met, and I tumbled head over heels, then stumbled flat on my face. How far can you go with a man who won't admit his own prejudice? And how many more men would humiliate me that way?

I began to miss the Northwest, the cool cleanliness of the air, the mountaintops like whipped cream in the sky. I missed the cobblestone alleys of Pike Place Market, my friends, the easy, casual atmosphere of Seattle.

Then Ma's business faltered, and one day her voice came through forlorn over the phone, and I knew I had to come back.

Now I take the long way home, walking the neighborhood to clear my head. So Ma has found me a man. She's so happy, and the happiness of others has always been my concern. As a child, I felt I could see people in other lives, in other possibilities. I could hear the longings of finches in the blackberry bushes, of the mice in the underbrush. I adopted stray cats and plastered stickers on our windows to the pine siskins from hitting the panes. I sat in the woods for hours, letting the needs and fears of animals climb into me, then helping where I could.

"How does she know where to find these creatures?" Ma asked once when I brought home a litter of kittens whose mother had been killed by a car. Their hunger and thirst and fear had screamed at me in my sleep. I found the fur-balls hidden in a hollow log in the woods. We nursed the kittens to health and adopted them out.

My parents didn't have the *knowing,* but they surmised that the gods had endowed me with increased sensitivity. I didn't begin to understand my own ability until the week after Christmas, in the third grade.

I had Miss America Barbie, the peach-colored doll with a smooth complexion, torpedo breasts out of proportion with her stilt-long legs, a glittering crown on her head. At recess my friends and I ran around the playground, the dolls' red satin capes trailing in the wind. Then a rock dropped and hit me in the head. I stumbled and fell.

I lay on my back, blinking at the open sky. I touched my forehead, expecting to find blood, but my fingers touched dry, unbroken skin. The rock had fallen into my head and lay smoking like a chunk of meteor. It wasn't a real rock. It was a feeling, a longing.

Someone stared down at me from the monkey bars—Leslie, a thin, quiet girl with light gray eyes. Her arm had brushed mine as she'd climbed, and I'd felt an inkling of the longing.

She smiled, revealing a big gap where her front tooth had gone missing. You couldn't tell by looking at her that the meteor of longing had come from her, that it had fallen from her mind into mine.

Miss America Barbie was still clutched in my right hand, but now her cape was muddy. A few boys gathered nearby, snickering. They were trying to peek up Leslie's skirt. She didn't seem to notice.

The smoking meteor sank into my brain, and I glimpsed, in fleeting images, Leslie's spindly Christmas tree at home, her parents fighting. She didn't get any dolls for Christmas, not even a book. She got hand-me-down clothes, and her heart ached for Miss America.

Why couldn't I see it in her face?

"Come down here, Leslie!" I called, and everyone turned to look.

Leslie climbed down the monkey bars, her eyes devouring Miss America.

I handed her the doll. "You can have her. She's yours."

Her eyes widened as she looked at the doll, then at me.

"I don't need your stupid doll," she said and threw it. Miss America splashed into a puddle. Her tiny, tailored dress was ruined, soggy and sagging.

Leslie retrieved her longing and marched away. I sat up,

and the kids gathered around, whispering and mumbling. A sour taste came into my mouth. I'd thought it would be easy to give Leslie what she wanted. Why had she thrown the doll and walked away? I could still feel her need.

I rescued the doll from the puddle.

Leslie avoided me after that. I was too young to understand the power of pride—and fear—that can make us turn away from what we want the most.

Soon after that, my father died while on a research trip to India. I don't remember grief. I remember flying to India for the memorial. I remember piles of steamed rice and dahl, concerned relatives pinching my cheeks and stuffing me with food. I remember my mother's tears.

Gradually, life returned to normal. I learned to wait in the shadows, to watch and learn before acting. And over the years, I learned that I could help in Ma's shop, bringing happiness to strangers by selecting the perfect sari for each of them. That way, I could disguise my intentions, and nobody would walk away in a huff, embarrassed by their own hidden longings.

My beauty blossomed gradually, creeping in and taking up residence in my body so insidiously that I barely noticed it. Like a retreating glacier, my childhood melted to reveal hidden abundance. My breasts grew to perfect proportions, my waist shrank, my legs extended into goddess legs, and my hair came in thick and lush, long and shiny. Other girls avoided me, and the boys stared. Once a bicyclist crashed into a telephone pole, knocked out two teeth and broke his nose, because he was paying more attention to me than the road ahead of him.

Sick with grief and guilt, I shaved my head, donned combat boots, and started wearing huge sunglasses and ripped jean jackets. Ma thought it was a teenage phase, but she didn't understand. A divine spotlight shone on me wherever I went.

Only now can I modulate my appearance, downplay it when I need to, let my hair down at opportune moments.

Now, in our modest saltbox house on the hill, only the soft, amorphous thoughts of squirrels and cats settle into my brain. I stop before going inside and survey the beveled windows, the stained glass catching the waning autumn sunlight. A plethora of salvaged shrubs and trees find refuge in our yard. I've taken such care with this garden, but when I marry, I shall have to leave, as all women do. I've been preparing for this, and yet my heart pounds a frantic beat.

Take deep breaths, Lakshmi. You're jumping to conclusions. You've not even met the man. All the answers will come.

I pick up the mail and go inside, relax at the familiar smell of this morning's tea, the wood scent of our home. Shiva greets me at the door, as usual, rubbing against my legs, purring. I scoop him up and bury my face in his gray striped fur. He settles into my arms and extends a front paw. Puffs of happiness emanate from him, and a vague relief. Every time we leave, he half believes we'll never come home.

"Where's Parvati, huh? Where's she hiding this time?" Parvati is my other Maine coon cat. Shiva and Parvati, the eternal lovers in Hindu mythology.

I scratch Shiva's ears, and he purrs louder. I don't see Parvati's whereabouts in his small, but complex mind. I never believed that smaller meant simpler. I've known since childhood that the tiniest field mouse survives with great skill and wit.

I let Shiva down, and he bats a ball of fluff, then follows me through the house, his purring engine at my feet.

I plunk the pile of mail on the dining table next to the newspaper, which sits in a mess beside my half-empty coffee cup, the soy milk congealed on top. Shiva jumps up on the newspaper, his favorite spot when I'm trying to read. He stares at me expectantly, images of grass and dewdrops filling his mind. Greenery, a symphony of tiny sounds unknown to humans, a rush of freedom and clean air and smells.

I keep calling Parvati in a gentle voice, and a faint commotion comes from the cabinet above the refrigerator. She steps out, blinking in the light like a queen roused from a royal nap.

"What are you doing up there, you silly thing?" I grab her and carry her to the floor before she finds her own dangerous way down.

While the cats eat, I check our voice mail. A message

from Ma's sister, inquiring about Ravi, and another crackling, long-distance message from Ma's mother, Nona, in India. So word is already out! A message from Samantha, from the homeless shelter, reminding me to bring in our clothing donations, and a message from my friend Mitra. "Remember you're having lunch with Nisha and me tomorrow. We'll pick you up at noon." Nisha and Mitra are my two best Indian friends from our undergraduate years at the University of Washington. We joined the Indian Students Union, met for lunch on Thursdays, and we've kept up the tradition ever since.

I smile and erase the message. I can't wait to tell them about my day, about Asha Rao and my prospects with Ravi Ganguli.

I go to my room, full of books and pictures of the goddess, and fire up my computer. My fingers tremble as I check my email. Many from cousins and friends, and spammers. And there it is, a message from Ravi Ganguli with a photograph attached.

> *Dear Lakshmi,*
>
> *I hope this finds you and your mother healthy and happy. I remember your father fondly from his visits to India. I was very small, but he remains in my memory. I remember your ma with great affection as well . . .*

He remembers Ma and Baba! I want to reach into the computer and touch Ravi Ganguli, ask him what he remembers of my father. I glance at the bedside table, where I keep an old black-and-white shot of Baba holding me on his lap, reading to me from a children's illustrated hardcover of *The Ramayana*. He looks so young and handsome, his hair slicked back, not a mark of age on his smooth, narrow face. My memories of him have begun to fade, and Ma's thoughts of him turn to angst-ridden shadows. But here is a man who remembers my father with affection.

. . . Just two weeks back, my parents received a letter from your mother, which included a lovely snap of you in your garden . . .

Ma, you devil! Two weeks ago? She must've sent the picture of me in the half-transparent kurta, my hair flying. That shot wasn't meant to leave this house. I'm blushing at the computer screen.

. . . and I must say that I found you the most breathtaking creature I've ever seen . . .

Most men do, when I'm not in my daytime disguise.

. . . I hope you do not consider me too forward. If your temperament is quite as radiant as your face, I

*should ask you to be my wife immediately. But
again, I march ahead of myself. I will be most honored to meet you when you come to India.*

Warmly yours,
Ravi Ganguli

His words send a thrill through me, and when I down-
load his picture, I can't stop staring at the slender, cultured man in the image. He's wearing a cream-colored
kurta and khaki pants. The kurta is embroidered with an
intricate gold pattern. What American man would wear
such an exotic shirt? He leans against a railing, a backdrop
of snowcapped peaks behind him. All residual baby fat has
burned away, leaving a regal, Maharaja-like face, a hint of
a beard shadowing his jaw. His eyes twinkle, and he's
about to laugh. I'm instantly jealous of the person taking
the picture, the person who knows what that laughter is
all about.

I hit the reply button and type.

Dear Mr. Ganguli,
  Many thanks for your kind, flattering message.
~~*I've now seen your snap and I must say, you are
handsome*~~

Scratch that. A woman can't be quite so forward in
India.

I'll be honored to meet you as well. . . .

I give him our address, hit the send button, and sign off in time to hear the kitchen door squeak open. Ma comes straight to my room and hovers over me.

"So, Bibu, has he written? You've made a plan to see him?"

"Yes, he wrote a nice letter."

"Brilliant!" Ma flops on my bed and stares at the ceiling, her eyes bright. "I've hoped and waited for this day, and how I wish your Baba could see you now, see what a wonderful daughter you are."

"Thank you, Ma, and you're a wonderful mother." I hug her and glance at the bright South Indian painting of the goddess Lakshmi above the bureau. In the swirls of colorful clouds around her, I see hope.

As I cook aloo gobi, chapatis, and dahl for supper, I wonder about Ravi. Is he a true gentleman? He'll love my cooking, love my ma, love Shiva and Parvati, love me. We'll have five boy babies, and all will be well. This is every Indian woman's dream, is it not? I close my eyes and imagine him coming up behind me, kissing my neck.

Ma stretches supper over two hours, as usual. Long after I've finished eating, I quietly read at the table while she works her way through the potato and cauliflower in the aloo gobi. Since Baba died, she expands the smallest details of life to fill extra time. When she's not working, she's eating or cleaning or poring over sari catalogs.

Usually I stay up with her, and sometimes I play the piano. I lose myself—and the *knowing*—in the symmetry of a Bach invention or a Chopin waltz. But tonight, I excuse myself and go to my room, take my journal from the bookshelf, and pull my father's fragile letter from between the pages. I imagine him wearing his woolen suit in the Himalayan foothills, his breath condensing into steam in the cold mountain air. He was probably whistling on the train. He always whistled. He was thinking of me. It was as if he knew what would happen.

> *My dearest Bibu,*
>
> *I wish you and your ma were here. I've just come from the city, now taking the train to Darjeeling to visit my closest friend, Dilip Ganguli, and his wife, Sangita. They have a bright son, Ravi, a little older than you. A good boy. Perhaps one day the two of you shall meet.*
>
> *Through the mists in the valleys, I see your little face asking me to read another page. I hope your ma is reading to you from* The Ramayana *and not just the* Curious George *and* Magician's Nephew. *I hope you are taking baths. You would love Darjeeling.*

Always take care of your ma, Bibu.
Remember, family is the most important thing.
                              With love and affection,
                                                    Baba

Always take care of your ma.
I am, Baba, as best I can.

These last words from my father, found intact in the wreckage of the train, with the address already on the letter, reached us in America by some miracle of mail. Perhaps my father knows whether Ravi is the man for me, whether Ma's shop will become world famous.

I wish my father would visit my dreams, but when I fall into slumber, he remains elusive, hiding in the cosmos, out of sight.

Five

The next morning, the store spins in a tizzy, as if the fabrics know they're going to be shaped into beautiful wedding costumes and they're all aglow, whispering among themselves. The walls blush with new excitement.

"This is the one," Mr. Basu says, doing the sideways head nod as he stocks shelves. His two hairs stand at attention on his shiny head. "This project will take us over the top. We'll be full of business. We'll be on the television, and then your ma will be famous. Asha Rao. The actress! I can hardly believe it!"

"Oh, Sanjay, stop babbling and work!" Ma rushes around straightening piles of saris, nearly knocking over customers.

I stock new arrivals, open bills, check inventory, phone messages.

"Did you see how beautiful she was?" Pooja says, cleaning coffee cups. She also brought pastries from Cedarlake Café. "But she's not as beautiful as Lakshmi."

Ma narrows her gaze at me. "You must not take off the glasses when Asha Rao is here—"

"You know I won't, Ma." I wink at her and she winks back. We're not mentioning Ravi Ganguli to anyone in the store just yet.

As I brush past a customer, an intense sadness hits me, the world drooping and melting, as if it's a massive ice cream cone left in the sun. The customer is a woman wrapped in a conservative dark green sari, the pallu over her head. An older woman marches after her—clearly her mother. "Sita! On the left. The saris on the left." Her mother points, and Sita turns left.

I rush up to her and take her hand, and I nearly burst into tears. Such sadness! Her skin is smooth, a gold-tinted brown. She's wearing no makeup, and her face is round and childish, although she must be in her twenties. Her nose is a button holding her features together.

"Can I help you?" I ask.

"Sita's getting married," her mother says, barging forward. "We need a wedding sari."

I'm still holding Sita's cool hand.

"Congratulations." I push the glasses up on my nose. Sita gives me a distant, underwater smile.

"Hurry up, Sita. We haven't got all day." Her mother barks her way through the store, pointing out this fabric, that fabric, this style, that style, and each time, Sita simply nods and complies. *She's miserable, can't you see?* I want to scream at her mother.

"We're all very proud of Sita," her mother's telling me. "She now has her degree, and we have found her a good man. I am ready for grandchildren."

"You're getting married here and not in India?" I say politely.

"Her grandmother is here, very ill, can't travel," the mother says. "The groom, however, is coming from India, and Sita will return with him. He's very rich, nah?" The mother smiles, and Sita looks at her sandals. If the carpet could reach up to pull her down, she would go gladly.

"I have to measure Sita," I say quickly, waving my trusty tape measure.

"Measure for a sari?" her mother says.

"Just in case she needs a custom-made blouse. We call in a very good seamstress—"

"Hurry up then. We haven't got all day," the mother says, and I'm ushering Sita into the dressing room.

"Did you agree to this match?" I whisper to her. "Are you in love?"

"Love is marriage," she says softly. "If a man is unwilling to marry you, it is not love."

"So you do love him?" I can't see far down into the murky water of her soul. Would I recognize true love if I saw it?

"My parents have chosen the right match for me."

Strict obedience is rare among the younger set these days, especially in America. "The world is changing, Sita. Maybe your parents would let you speak your mind. If you're not sure—"

"Why wouldn't I be? And it's not for me to say." She lifts her arms and dutifully lets me measure her.

"What about this fiancé? How did you meet him?"

Someone pounds on the dressing room door.

"Just a moment—we're almost finished," I shout. We haven't got much time.

"At his parents' house in Mumbai," Sita says. I see a dark, damp flat—the power has been cut, the monsoon dampness creeps into every corner. In the narrow streets, people have abandoned their cars. Empty Ambassadors float along filthy rivers that once were roads. Sita's family has taken hours to get here, and her fiancé, a handsome man with unusually wide shoulders and silver hair, comes out and takes her hand. Two sets of parents are there, and a hollowness moves through her.

"What will happen when you return to India?" I ask.

"Kishor and I will live with his family," she says. "His mother wants a grandson. She has three children and no grandchildren yet."

"And you're going to give her one."

"Or two." Her mind has gone dark, as if her mother has intruded and snuffed out a candle. I'm still holding Sita's arm when her mother barges in.

"Let's go," she says. "Come, Sita—what's all this talking?"

"I'll be just another moment," I say. "If you could wait outside, please."

Her mother steps outside with a huff.

I try to imagine the fabric that could calm Sita, a sari that could carry her across the threshold into a better future. "It won't be so bad," I say. "Everyone gets scared of marriage, but I'm sure you'll be happy."

Her smile wavers like a mirage. "Thank you."

"Your fiancé looks very— I mean, he must be a good man," I say. "And you miss India, no?"

She nods, and I see the right sari for her. Slippery chiffon orange. I don't know why it will work, but I sense the warmth that it will bring her.

"If you ever need to talk to someone. Day or night. Call me," I say. "My home number's also in the telephone book."

Sita gets up, an automaton stepping out to greet her mother, and I find my fingers trembling.

I hand the orange chiffon sari to her mother. "It's not a wedding sari, Mrs.—"

"Dutta. What's this orange?"

"Important for building her trousseau. I also have a wedding sari." I show her a shimmering ruby-red sari that changes hue when viewed from different angles.

"Ah, lovely!" Mrs. Dutta and Sita gasp in unison.

Mrs. Dutta pays, grabs both saris, and strides out, her daughter close behind.

I go back into the office to catch my breath. Frightened brides have blown into the shop before, carried on the northwest winds. Tastes of the exotic, memories of India, images of gold and jewels and love and kisses. Pulsing hearts, roses bursting with fragrance. Hope and children and white picket fences, enormous wedding parties and priests adorned with garlands—all of these images have passed through, travelers on their way to future lives. I've held the hands of brides, guided them through the fear and into bliss.

But have I done my best to help Sita? Will the orange sari work?

"Bibu, what are you doing hiding back here, nah?" Ma bursts in, her face flushed, eyes shining. "Hurry up and come out—Asha is here with her driver!"

Six

Asha Rao is back in the store, and I'm trapped in an invisible bubble that keeps the *knowing* outside. Someone—maybe the goddess—blew that bubble and is now secretly laughing at me. *Ha-ha. Now see how well you survive with only your five senses. Ha!* But Helen Keller survived without sight or sound. If she could do it, I can make it without the *knowing*.

I push the glasses up on my nose and stride forward to take Ms. Rao's cool, delicate hand. The driver is in a navy blue suit that brings out the startling blue of his eyes; his long blond hair is slicked back.

I focus on Asha's delicate expressions, her movements, the shift of her eyes, her words, for I have no *knowing* to guide me.

The driver curls his fingers around the wheelchair handles and pushes Asha around the room in that effortless way, as if he could push a house.

Mr. Basu comes running from the back and stops in the middle of the room.

"Oh, gods!" he exclaims and presses his hands to his cheeks. "The leak has come again!" As if the leaky pipe under the bathroom sink is an unwelcome cousin. The two hairs on his head are drooping, portending foul weather.

Across the room, Ma's face freezes in a proprietary smile.

"Oh, no," I breathe and hurry back to stifle Mr. Basu. "What's going on?" I whisper. "If it's just the drip—"

"Puddles on the floor," Mr. Basu says with great sadness, as if a monsoon has swept away his family.

I step closer, grab Mr. Basu's arm. "Get the handyman."

"His wife says he's working in Bellingham."

"Then call the plumber. Have him come in the back way."

"Plumber's busy, Lakshmi."

"Damn it." I rarely use such words. I glance back toward Ma and Pooja, dancing like consorts around the Bollywood goddess. Our position is precarious. Nick stands near the counter, scanning the shop, hands behind his back. I turn to Mr. Basu. "Do whatever you can to fix it."

Then Nick is beside me. "Problem?"

I step away, putting a protective distance between this enormous man and me.

"No problem, no problem." Mr. Basu scratches his head. "We've got a leak."

I cringe. "We can take care of it," I say. "Small drip."

"Huge ocean," Mr. Basu says. "All over, all over, it will be flooding into the office next."

"It's nothing." I push Mr. Basu back toward the office, trying to stuff him in there the way I stuff saris into boxes, but he stands his ground.

"Making gushing sound," he says. "Something new." He's always offering unnecessary information.

"Oh, Mr. Basu!" My face heats.

"Let me take a look," Nick says.

"No need," I say.

"Yes, look, look!" Mr. Basu turns, and Nick follows him into the back office. I'm right behind them, my heart fluttering in funny, fast beats. "It's really not necessary—"

But he's already moving through the office, his bulk incongruous in the small space. Mr. Basu is leading him past the piles of paper on my desk, the pictures of family, the half-eaten sandwiches, the dirty coffee machine, and into the bathroom, which also needs to be cleaned, my lotion sitting on the sink, a box of tampons on the toilet tank. It's like having a stranger in your house when you haven't had time to tidy up.

"Got tools?" Nick asks. How can he be so calm when there's a steady but thin stream of water pouring from the cabinet below the sink?

"Tools?" Mr. Basu and I say in unison.

"Yeah, tools. You know, wrenches and screwdrivers."

"Tools in janitor's closet," Mr. Basu says.

"We'll call our handyman," I say. "No need to—"

"I can handle it," Nick says.

Mr. Basu disappears and returns with a red metal box, the tools clanking around inside, weighing down his arm. Nick takes the box and holds it with ease, as if it's a loaf of bread. Ma rushes in, and her eyes widen. "Oh, no! What's happened in here, Bibu?" She looks at me, then at Nick, and her brows furrow with disapproval. "What's he doing here?"

"He's offered to help, Ma."

"What have you done, Bibu?" Her voice has a serrated edge.

"I didn't do it!" I shout.

Ma's eyes narrow at me. "Call the plumber."

Mr. Basu gives her the spiel, while Nick gives me a half smile, those blue eyes amused. I'm wearing glasses and a ponytail, like a schoolgirl, and my mother is calling me Bibu, and we're standing in a lake in our messy bathroom. Well, Mr. Nick, see how much time you have for house-cleaning when you have to balance the books, stock saris, measure customers for custom-made outfits, and grin at the Mrs. Dasguptas of the world all day. Never mind trying to find a perfect Bengali husband and catapult the shop into the Fortune 500 in the next three months.

"I can fix it, ma'am," Nick says, shifting his gaze to my mother.

"Thank you," Ma breathes, and then her gaze dismisses him. "We'll pay you appropriately."

I'm thrown back to India, where Ma renders rickshaw drivers invisible with a wave of her hand.

Nick puts the toolbox on the toilet seat, whips off his jacket, and rolls up his sleeves to reveal muscular arms with a hint of blue tattoos beginning above both elbows. Tattoos? What kind of man is this?

Mr. Basu brings a pile of towels and we mop the floor.

Nick gets down on his back on a towel, easing himself into the cabinet.

The phone rings shrilly, drilling through my ears.

"I'll get it." Ma waves an arm at Mr. Basu, and they both disappear into the shop.

"Do you always fix plumbing wherever you go?" I ask Nick.

"If the pipes break," he says in a muffled voice. "Hand me that screwdriver."

I kneel and peer into the cabinet. As he messes with the pipes, his sleeves ride up his arms, revealing muscles and more of the tattoos—one barbed wire, the other a dream catcher.

Did the tattoos hurt? Did he show off to his girlfriend? He must lift weights with those muscular arms.

Translucent suds of emotion fizz in the air, but they're not coming from Nick.

They're coming from me!

What's going on? What does this mean? I've never seen bubbles like this. For a crazy moment, I'm sure he can see the pink foam surrounding me.

"Pass me that wrench," he says. "Ms. Sen?"

"Oh, sorry!" I fumble in the toolbox.

"That one on the left."

I hand him the wrench.

He finishes screwing something on and the water stops flowing from the pipe, just like that. He slides out of the cabinet and stands, looking bigger than he did when he walked in.

"You're really good at fixing things," I say.

"I fix whatever breaks at my parents' place all the time," Nick says. "My dad's not the greatest with tools."

"Even our handyman takes hours, and he doesn't seem to know what he's doing. Not that you're a handyman. That's not what I meant."

"No problem. I found this in the pipe." He hands me a golden ring, untarnished and glinting in the light. For an awkward moment, it feels as if he's proposing to me.

I bring the ring close to my face. A few stray bubbles float by. "Wow—looks like pure gold. I wonder who lost this."

"Could be a wedding ring." He peers closer, the scent of his metallic aftershave in my nose.

"Initials *J. T.* in English. I can't read this part, see? Words engraved into the inside. Looks like Sanskrit! Maybe it's my mother's, or she knows whose it is."

"I love a good mystery." Nick grins as he presses a business card into my hand. "Let me know what you find out."

"Why? Do you want to keep the ring?"

"Finders keepers?" Now he's smiling.

"I suppose you're right. You found the ring."

But I can't help thinking he gave me the card for another reason. *Nick Dunbar, Dunbar Limousine Service.* With a telephone number. I glance into his eyes, catching a glimpse of promise. He sees past the glasses, past the baggy shirt and my severe hairstyle.

"Thanks for fixing the . . . pipe," I call after him as he leaves.

Seven

After Asha and Nick leave, the bubbles pop, but I'm not back to normal. I've entered an unmapped territory with unknown suds lurking in the shadows. I'm spent, shaky, disoriented.

The *knowing* returns gradually, but why did it leave again? Is the goddess testing me?

"Oh, what shall we do?" Mr. Basu presses his hands to his cheeks. "So much more work! Fittings and stitchings—"

"Hush, Sanjay. This is all good!" Ma rushes around straightening saris, smoothing kameezes. "We'll take it one step at a time. We must order more jewelry."

I remember the ring. "Ma, I want to show you something."

In the office, I show her the ring.

"Where did you find this?" Her face goes hard.

"Nick found it in the pipe under the sink."

"Ah, the driver," Ma says dismissively.

"Is it yours? The initials are *J. T.*"

Her lips form a tight line. A hint of anger touches her eyes and is gone. "I know nothing about this. You can throw it away."

"Throw it away! But Ma, it's gold, and it has this etching too—"

"I don't know about any etching."

But I'm sure she does. She's distracted the rest of the morning, putting saris on the wrong shelves, walking away from customers halfway through conversations.

At lunchtime, Mitra shows up in her VW Bug to take me to the Cosmos Café for lunch. A long-haired, dark-skinned Kathak dancer, she exudes compact efficiency, but her wild streak hovers close to the surface, in the silver stud through her nose, in her carefree driving style. I've known her for nine years, and she has always been reckless. And she has always loved Kathak, her one thread of connection to her Indian culture. *Katha* means "story," and traditional Kathak dance always weaves a tale in elaborate, precise movements as old as time, as delicate as butterfly wings. Her feet move so quickly, tap-tapping the stage, enormous silver bells called *ghunghrus* clanging on her ankles.

"You'll get us both killed," I scream as she cuts across two lanes of traffic.

She ignores me as usual. "You look flushed. Are you sick? I hope you're not catching the cold that's going around—"

"Look at the road, not at me!"

"Or maybe that sixth sense of yours went into hyper-drive?"

I tell her about Ravi Ganguli, Asha Rao, the ring in the drainpipe. "And the weird thing was, the *knowing* disappeared."

"Are you reading me now?"

"I'm not a two-bit fortune-teller, Mitra. I can't read you at will."

The car swerves to the left, then back into her lane. Mitra parks in the lot behind the café, the car sprawled at an angle across two spaces. "Your ma must know about the ring," she says. "Can't you read her mind and find out—"

"There are limits to what I see," I say. "I've never seen all the way into her. She thinks I have heightened intuition, and that's all."

"There's some sordid family secret in that ring, I'm telling you."

"We don't have any family secrets."

"Everyone does." Mitra frowns, and her mind wanders away to a backyard patio near the beach, where a small girl dances in a tiny yellow silk Kathak costume, her black hair flying. The skirt flares out at the bottom, and she looks like miniature sunshine when she spins. Her heart is so full that her happiness spills onto the beach and makes the seashells smile.

A tall man watches from a lawn chair. He smiles and claps, proud of his young daughter. Soft water laps the shore, and a seagull cries, following in the wake of a ferry steaming ashore in West Seattle. Every time the girl bangs her feet on the patio, the bells on her ankles clanging in metallic song, the man encourages her, so she dances faster and faster.

Then a phantom hand reaches from the sea and sucks the man into the surf, and I'm plummeting back to reality, Mitra tugging my sleeve. "Earth to Lakshmi! You were off in la-la land."

"Did you ever own a yellow Kathak costume with paisley on it when you were a little girl?"

An invisible veil covers her eyes. "I don't remember. Did you have some kind of vision?"

"I just caught a glimpse of someone. I thought she might've been you."

"What else did you see?"

"You were on the beach." Instinct tells me not to mention the man, probably her father. I know she hasn't spoken to him in four years, since she refused to study medicine or marry the man he chose for her.

"We lived near Alki beach." She drums her fingers on the steering wheel. "I've always loved it there. I could watch the ferries come in. That's all you saw?"

"That's all."

"But why now? Did you reach into my head and pull out my memories or something?"

"You know I can't control what I see. You seemed very happy there. You were dancing."

"What else are you seeing now? What am I thinking?"

"You're craving a hot fudge sundae with bananas and whipped cream."

She laughs. "But my waistline will have to make do with a Greek salad, dressing on the side."

We go inside to meet Nisha. The café caters to an eclectic Northwest crowd, some in suits, others in sandals and flannel shirts. A group of wiry bicyclists gathers at a corner table, their tight spandex outfits outlining every body part. The acidic scent of coffee clings to the air, and the walls are covered with Native Northwest art—carved wooden orcas, a Haida ceremonial mask, a hazy watercolor image of Mount Rainier rising above the Puget Sound.

We find Nisha at a table by the window, her sculpted chin turned toward the expansive view of the lake. Even as the clouds promise more rain, parents are out pushing jogging strollers, Rollerblading, or simply walking. Nisha looks as if she does all three. Everything about her is slim and healthy, studied and planned, even the way she smoothes her blue power suit and sips her wine.

Two years ago, she returned to India for a perfect arranged marriage, and now she and her husband live in a mansion in North Seattle. They're blissfully happy, and beneath her manicured demeanor, she has a heart the size of the universe. She's a successful banker who donates to nearly every nonprofit in the city. She convinced me to give several saris for charity fund-raisers.

We bring her up to speed and order our salads. I produce the ring, much admired around the table.

"Must be a sign," Nisha says. "Your marriage will come soon."

"I wish I could read the inscription," I say.

"It's something cryptic, a big secret." Mitra waves down the waiter, and we place our orders. "Terribly exciting," she goes on.

"You're such a drama queen," Nisha says. "Always seeing something big and dramatic in everyday happenings. The ring slipped off someone's finger and fell down the sink, that's all." She turns her water glass between her hands in a distracted way.

Mitra snorts. "Who got up grouchy today? You and that husband of yours need a vacation. Drive down to Portland for a romantic weekend. You're always working!"

"I guess I'm cranky," Nisha says. "I've been working

long hours, and Rakesh made partner at the firm. He doesn't have much time for vacations, but . . . we're planning a trip to Baja soon, if he can get away. He's got a big case that might go to trial."

The waiter brings our salads and soups, and we dig into our lunches. I am grateful for the distraction, but the *knowing* is hyperactive, and I catch a glimpse of Nisha running along a narrow alley in darkness, a green sari flapping around her, tears in her eyes. Then the image disappears. What could it mean?

I try to focus on the restaurant, on strangers absorbed in intimate conversations. A gaunt woman sits across from a man who gesticulates in animated movements. She's wearing a woolen cap decorated with a golden broach, and her eyelashes and eyebrows are missing. Her skin has a pale, brittle appearance, but her eyes shine with life as her companion talks, and then Mitra returns to my thoughts unbidden. She's the little girl again, dancing, only her father is much older and thinner, bent forward, and then Mitra grows older and suddenly I know what's happening now, so many years later.

Mitra's father is dying.

Eight

"How are your parents?" I say in the car on the way back to the shop.

"My ma's great, taking singing and yoga classes." Mitra drives with unusual caution, staying in her lane.

"Your dad?"

"What about him? He's a jerk." Her eyes brighten, and she blinks rapidly.

"I saw him. I think he may be ill."

She sniffs and turns up the radio to a blaring volume.

I turn it down again. "Talk to me, girl. Don't keep this from me."

"I didn't want to tell you, because, you know." Her fingers grip the steering wheel, and she slams on the brake, nearly running a red light. Speckles of rain hit the windshield.

"Because my father died? That was a long time ago, Mitra."

"There's nothing to talk about." At the green light, she turns left around the lake, not waiting for oncoming traffic. An angry motorist beeps his horn and gives Mitra the finger. She gives him the finger back.

"You haven't seen him lately, have you?" I say as she parks at the curb in front of the shop. "Not in four years."

She shakes her head, her hands still gripping the steering wheel. "I talk to Mom. My sister's staying there now."

"Why can't you go and see him?"

She turns to me, her face an open wound. "Don't you remember? He disowned me. I told him I wasn't going to medical school, that I was going to teach dance and perform full-time, that I was going to try to make it as an artist, and you know what he said? He said he didn't have a daughter anymore. He wouldn't talk to me, return my calls. Nothing!"

I hug her, her strong, wiry body rigid with anger. "Mitra, he can't help it. He's just who he is. He loves you. He loves your dancing. I saw it in his eyes. I felt it."

"No, you don't know. In Indian families love is conditional, Lakshmi. Kids have been ostracized, kicked out of families, totally disowned for all kinds of reasons."

"I know, but you have to be brave. You have to trust."

Tears run down her face now, and her nose is red. "I should've expected what I got. That he would hate me."

"He doesn't hate you. I think he's . . . sad. I think he misses you. I think he wants to put all this aside—"

"Oh, stop it! How can you possibly know that, Lakshmi? You're not there. He doesn't want to talk to me ever again. To him, I don't exist."

I give her a squeeze, then open the door. "I'm sorry, Mitra. Remember, family is the most important thing. I'm sure he knows that. Why don't you invite him to your next performance? The one at the Studio Theater? I'm sure he'll be thrilled to come."

"No, he won't."

"Think about it. Please."

She sighs but says nothing.

When I get out of the car, she screeches away, leaving a trail of white exhaust in her wake. But the image of the yellow costume remains, and I know what I have to do. I go inside to find a similar fabric, and then I pull Mitra's measurements from our files and put a call in to the seamstress.

The rest of the afternoon, I can't concentrate. My mind whirls with images from the minds of my friends and customers, and at home that evening, Ma chatters about our upcoming trip to India, and I nod and murmur at all the right moments.

At supper, she presses a hand to my forehead. "You're flushed. Do you have a fever?" I deny it, say I had a long day.

"You mustn't be sick in India, Bibu, makes your face look blotchy and pasty."

"I'm fine, Ma." Just heavy with the weight of my friends' problems.

"You must eat only good foods before we go, and not all the time the coffee in the mornings."

"I love coffee, Ma."

"We must take only the best saris for you—"

"We have plenty of saris."

"And not all the time doing the Jane Fonda–type aerobics and walking everywhere. You'll become too thin."

"Jane Fonda is so eighties, Ma. I love walking to work."

"Then eat more sweets and pastries and such to balance it out." She goes on about my teeth, about my speech patterns. "Try to have a bit of Bengali accent, nah? Then he'll know you have not completely lost the language."

I rub Ma's arm. "You know I haven't. You know I love you more than anything."

She touches my cheek. "I know, Bibu. Your father is gazing upon us from the heavens and smiling. Finally, smiling. I can feel his happiness."

"Yes, Ma."

After supper, I find a new email message from Ravi Ganguli:

Dear Lakshmi,

    I look forward to returning to Seattle. I studied as an exchange student at the University of Washington for one year, and I grew to love the Pacific Northwest. It will be an honor to see the city sights again, but this time with you. Although we haven't met, I feel as though I know you. I enclose a snap taken at Discovery Park.

                    Yours with affection,
                           Ravi

He includes a photograph of himself in a Seattle Mariners T-shirt and jeans, his hair tousled, arms around two other men, one blond, the other red-haired. They're young, maybe twenty, laughing, their faces flushed, a field of grass and pine trees stretching behind them. A strip of ocean glints in the background. Ravi's lean face is open and accessible. Handsome. A man I want to know. His Indianness remains an unchanging, timeless glow emanating from him. And yet, he fits in smoothly in the American scene. I want to be there in that picture, in the past with him.

I send a wistful reply asking if he's ever ridden the elevator up the Space Needle to Seattle's highest lookout, whether he likes the ferry, the fish-throwers in Pike Place Market. I sign the note, *With anticipation, Lakshmi Sen.*

There's a note from Pooja, giving the time and place of her wedding rehearsal next weekend. I nearly forgot! *Maybe I should marry Asha Rao's driver instead,* she jokes, adding a smiley face to her message. She signs, *Your cold-footed friend, Pooja.*

I send her a pep talk and take the golden ring and Nick Dunbar's business card from my purse. I have a crazy idea. I flip open my cell phone and punch in his number. My heartbeat picks up. At nine o'clock, I'll probably get his answering service, but I'm surprised when his deep, male voice comes on the line. "Dunbar Limousine."

"Is this Mr. Dunbar?" Of course it is. No mistaking that voice.

"That's me. Can I help you?"

"This is Lakshmi, from the sari shop. Remember me? You fixed our sink?" My voice trembles oddly.

"Hey, Lakshmi, what can I do for you?" I hear a radio or television in the background, people cheering on a sports channel. "Did you find out who lost the ring?"

"No, not yet! Um, I'd like to hire you, actually. If you have a little free time with all the driving you're doing for Asha Rao."

"What do you have in mind?"

"I want to surprise a friend. I want you to drive her in style—her and me, actually—to a very special event."

Nine

"This small golden kurta will be perfect for your baby girl!" I tell a new mother the next day at work. She's holding a pudgy, rosy-cheeked toddler on her hip. Cotton-puffs of pure bliss float from the child as she plays with her mother's long braid.

"For Diwali celebration, it's not too bright? Not too heavy?" The mother runs the fabric between her fingers.

"Very soft, perfect for a baby's skin," I say. "And not too bright for Diwali." The Indian festival of lights, to celebrate the New Year, is always a spectacular winter event, complete with parties, dances, and recitals.

Ma comes at me in a breathless jog. "Asha just called. You must take the fabric samples to her on the set today.

She hasn't time to come to the shop. They're filming in a house in Queen Anne. Have you gathered the fabrics? She wants only silk!"

"I had all kinds of fabric ready," I say.

"Only silk."

The baby giggles, pulling her mother's hair.

"I'll have to take your car," I say. "I walked again today."

"No need. Asha's sending a car." Ma glances at her watch. "Work quickly."

"She's sending a car?" I glance down at my brown, frumpy shirt, at my baggy jeans.

"It's already on the way."

"Here, Ma. Can you help with this Diwali costume?" I hand her the golden kurta.

"Oh, what a lovely child!" Ma exclaims.

I duck away, tuck back a few strands of stray hair. I don't even have time to apply lipstick. I have time only to stuff a variety of fabric samples into a large, flat briefcase before Nick strides in wearing a dark gray suit over an open-collared white shirt, his longish blond hair slicked back and damp, as if he's just washed it. The *knowing* spirals away, deflating like an unlucky balloon.

All eyes turn—maybe the customers expect Asha Rao, but then I realize it's not Asha they're looking at but Nick. Is he the one stealing the *knowing*? Even the baby gives him a dimply, toothless smile.

"Lakshmi, are you ready to go?" Ma asks in an anxious voice.

"The car's right outside," Nick says in a smooth, professional tone.

I stuff the last of the fabrics into the briefcase, grab my jacket, and follow him out to the car. He drove a white limousine today, not black, and he opens the passenger-side door for me.

"I'm sitting beside you?" I ask.

"Easier to talk," he says.

I hesitate, then slide into the front seat next to him. I put the briefcase on the seat between us, and yet Nick's presence takes up the whole car.

He reaches over to pull the shoulder belt across my lap, his arm barely brushing my breast, and in that instant, time stops. Then he clicks the seat belt into place, sits back in the driver's seat, and pulls smoothly into the road.

"So you keeping the big pickup a secret from your friend Pooka?" he asks.

"Pooja," I say. "I don't want her to know, so don't say anything."

"My lips are sealed."

"Thanks so much for doing this—and for giving me a discount."

"Hey—I don't do this just for the money." He switches

on the radio and whistles softly to "I Can See Clearly Now." He has perfect pitch.

"I never learned to whistle," I say. Where did that come from?

"I've heard you humming in the store," Nick says.

"Me, humming?" I blush. "I guess I've been too busy to notice."

"Have you always worked there?"

"Not always—after my father died, my mother couldn't bear to stay at her job. That was twenty years ago. So she opened the shop."

"You were just a kid."

"Yeah—I hung around the shop after school. My parents had both been teaching at South Cascade University. My father was a scholar, an editor of sacred Sanskrit texts. My mother has a master's in design. Baba left us some money, and so she started the business by herself. She's always been somewhat adventurous, trying new things. She took flute lessons for a while, then rappelling, if you can believe it."

Why am I divulging so much? Maybe the lull of the car, Nick's casual driving style, the warmth and comfort of the air are functioning like a truth serum to get me to talk.

"Cool lady, your mom," he says. "I'm sorry about your dad. Looks as though you're doing pretty well for yourself now."

"We're doing great," I lie. "But I haven't always worked

at the shop. I took time off to get my business degree at the UW, and I even worked in New York for three years."

"What brought you back?"

Ma's business was faltering. Sean and I broke up. "I missed my friends." That much is true. "Now I own half the store." I've already given far too much information to this driver. "So have you always driven a limousine?"

"Drove professionally for a while. Raced, gave it up while the money was good."

"You raced? Isn't that dangerous? Like a big adrenaline rush or death wish or something?"

"A bit of both. I got to know where all the best tracks are, where you can get your car driving sideways along a wall."

"I can't imagine driving sideways." I shiver. "I'd be afraid of flipping over."

"You feel the fear, and you go with the rush. But . . . I got older. I'm thirty-three now, an old man." He laughs.

"Do you do this all day, every day? Driving people like Asha Rao? Celebrities and such?"

"Hell no. There's more to life. Good food, sleep, a good workout. Baseball, football. Sex."

I bite my lip and pretend to look out the window, at the freeway rushing by, Seattle high-rises growing closer. "Tell me about your tattoos," I say quickly, to change the subject. "Where did you get them?"

"Oh, you noticed them, eh? Osaka. I was on liberty, a

long time ago. Can't you tell? My hair is long. Guys who had to wear their hair short always rebel and grow it long when they get out."

He'd look great in a uniform. Good in a suit, in jeans. He's a driver, I remind myself. Like rickshawallas or family chauffeurs. He's not even Indian.

"Why would you want to permanently deface your skin?" I ask. "Tattoos never come off, you know."

"Yeah, I thought about that. What if I'm a different person ten years from now? Lucky I didn't put a girlfriend's name on my arm."

I clear my throat. "So you have a girlfriend?" I ask politely.

"On and off. Her name is Liz. My mom keeps pushing me to tie the knot, but I'm not quite ready for that."

A memory stings me—of Sean saying exactly the same thing. *Not quite ready to tie the knot.* "So you have family around here?"

"My parents are still in Port Westwood, out near Port Gamble, Port Townsend, that area. They're retired, traveling all the time. Mother was a teacher, and a master gardener! My father's a businessman. Started Dunbar Limousine. I'm the eldest. I have two brothers and a sister. Youngest brother's a lawyer, sister's a teacher. My other brother and I run the business."

"It must be nice to have such a large immediate family," I say wistfully. "I've always wished for a sister or a brother, to take some of the burden off me. I feel such a tremendous responsibility to my mother, you know? She's lonely, and she puts all her energy into this man she found for me—"

"What man?" Nick gives me a sharp look as he exits the freeway in downtown Seattle.

"He's in India. We're going there in two weeks so I can meet him. We were planning to stay a while, but now that Asha has hired us, we're going for only a week. Can you imagine, going all the way around the world for only a week? I have a lot to do before we leave, and Pooja and Mr. Basu will have to hold down the fort while we're gone."

"Why do you have to go to India to meet a man? No men good enough for you here?" He's joking, but he sounds half-serious.

"I've gone out with a lot of different men," I say. "I guess I'm looking to settle down too. With the right guy."

The car climbs the hill into Queen Anne. "How will you know if he's the right one?"

I fall silent. That's a good question. Will pretty Valentine's Day hearts pop out of me? Out of Ravi? "Our parents matched us up using bio-data from our portfolios."

"What the hell is a bio-data portfolio?" Nick turns into an upscale residential district. "Is that like match.com?"

"Sort of—but we're matched up based on several criteria such as education, age, background."

"And that leads to true love." Nick's voice has a faint sour edge.

"I don't know. It might," I say curtly.

"We're here." He parks in front of a large, gray, pretentious, box-style home with ornate windows. Several trucks are parked along the curb, and a Seattle's Best coffee cart is set up at the foot of the driveway.

I sit motionless, suddenly seized by unease. "This is a movie set?" I ask. There is no stage, no lighting system, only men and women in jeans and T-shirts milling about, carrying electronic equipment up and down the steps. A few other people stand around doing nothing.

"Most of the time it's a waiting game," Nick says. "They spend half the day just setting up the lighting. Come on, I'll take you in." He carries my briefcase and leads me upstairs into the house, and I nearly trip over several cords. Cameras are set up on wheels in the hallway, and a slim woman in a black suit is talking excitedly with a tall, handsome blond man with a heavily made-up face. He's holding a script in his hands and listening to her intently.

There's a vibrant sense of camaraderie and excitement here, as people mill about directing each other and adjusting lights on an ornate living room scene.

I feel insubstantial in the chaos, like a puff of floating dust.

"Who's that blond man?" I whisper to Nick.

"He's Asha's leading man. They don't get along too well—she's down the hall, trying to stay away from him."

"And she has to pretend she's in love with him in the movie, right?"

Nick nods. "It's a hoot to watch them. On the set, they're in love, and off the set, they're at each other's throats."

The true lives of movie stars, invisible when the camera is rolling.

I follow Nick down the hall to a room filled with an elaborate display of catered finger foods, sandwiches, and drinks. Asha's sitting on a plush red couch, dressed in a white, revealing sari, the *choli* shirt so short that her entire midriff shows. She has her broken leg propped up on a stool. Her makeup adds a whole new layer to her face, a nearly clownlike, exaggerated flair. A diminutive woman with a severe hairstyle sits at a desk next to her.

"Blast these lines!" Asha shouts, holding her script. "How long do we have to wait to film again?"

"They're still working on the lights in the sitting room," the petite woman says with an English accent.

"Ah, Lakshmi!" Asha gives me a brilliant smile, glinting white teeth, and makes an expansive gesture. "Do sit down and put the samples here on the table. I haven't much time."

I turn to find Nick gone. Surprisingly, I feel adrift with-

out him. The *knowing* floats back into me in faint images—
Asha wanting to slap her leading man. Her English assistant
wanting lunch.

Here's my chance. I open the briefcase on the table. In
my frumpy getup, I look plain next to Asha. Her assistant
watches me in silence. There's a lot of shouting and moving
of heavy objects going on down the hall. I want to be there,
watching and listening.

Asha thumbs through the fabric samples with a distracted air. "For my assistant Ella here, what do you recom-
mend? Where are the chiffons?"

"You told me to bring only silk," I say. "I chose our best
patterns."

The diminutive woman clears her throat.

"She might look good in this," I say as I produce a thin,
tightly woven off-white piece with a matte texture.

"Chiffon is slimming," Asha says. "Try chiffon."

"I brought only the silks," I say again, my heart pounding. I unroll the fabrics on the table, on the carpet, and
Asha examines them all, asking questions about the slimming effects of the colors, how they'll go with other colors.
Ella disappears and returns with tea, and a bearded man
pops his head in. "About twenty minutes, Ms. Rao, okay?"

"You people are far too slow!" Asha waves a jewel-
beringed hand, and the bangles on her wrist make a tin-
kling sound. The man disappears.

"I'm stuck here with a group of lazy imbeciles who accomplish nothing all day," Asha says, rolling her eyes at me. "I'm sure you understand."

I give her a weak smile. "So, the fabrics—"

"I like these, but I was rather hoping for the chiffons—"

"Those are for more casual occasions—"

"Well, I want to see them," she says and laughs. "You'll go back and gather some of the other materials."

"Today? But—"

"I'll come by your shop. I have to practice my lines now. We've spent far too much time on this, and besides, Vijay should be with me to select the fabric and put in his share of the work. I have to prepare for the scene in which my American lover introduces me to his family. Can you imagine, we're preparing a whole day for this five-minute scene?"

"I didn't realize!"

"Shooting a film is all about preparation," Asha says. "One must be patient, but I haven't an ounce of patience left in my bones."

"Of course, that's understandable."

"Is it? And they give us the most bland food—this salmon pâté and Northwest chocolates. And biscuits. I need some spice, something to sting the tongue! Ugh, what a bore."

"I could see about arranging—"

ANjALI BANERJEE

"Nah, nah. This is not your concern."

I start to gather up the samples, and I realize that Asha could dismiss them all with the wave of her magic hand. She could order a feast for a hundred people, then send it to the garbage with a sneer, and nobody would complain.

I know that these silks will work, but she doesn't believe me, and really, my *knowing* is not what she wants. Asha is beautiful, talented, and slivers of honesty and generosity glimmer inside her, but she lacks . . . sensitivity. She looks at people and sees nothing but the reflection of herself. She doesn't see the real Ella, hidden behind her competence, trapped inside the gray business suit. Ella admires Asha with a deep, respectful reverence. And Asha has no idea. She will keep yelling at Ella, abusing her, and she will never know.

Frustration rises inside me. Ella helps Asha move from the couch to her wheelchair, then pushes her out of the room without a word, leaving me to gather up my fabric samples. I'm muttering angrily to myself when I notice Nick standing in the doorway.

"How long have you been here?" I ask.

"Long enough." There's a smile in his eyes. "Come on, I'll take you back to the shop."

For once, I'm grateful for the lack of *knowing* when I'm around Nick. I can hide in a blissfully quiet room of my own.

In the car, I throw the briefcase onto the seat, lean back, and close my eyes. The limousine is a lullaby.

"Have a good visit?" he asks, pulling out into traffic.

"I didn't realize how difficult it can be to work for Asha."

"She's demanding," he says, driving down through a dense neighborhood of Victorians and Craftsman-style bungalows. "But don't let it get to you."

"I put together all these samples, and she dismissed the whole lot. She asked for silk and then acted as if she didn't!"

"That's Asha. She changes with any shift in the wind," Nick says. "Hell, she's dismissed all her assistants when she doesn't like them."

"She does?" I cast him a worried look. "What about Ella?"

"She'd fire her in a heartbeat."

"Poor Ella. She really admires Asha."

"I admire you. I'd like to see you again."

I'm flaming red. "That won't be possible. I told you— I'm going to India."

"Maybe you don't have to go all that way."

I cross my arms over my chest. This man is annoying, and far too forward. When we get back, I thank him quickly and dash back into the store, my legs trembling. The *knowing* rushes back into me, but I find I'm longing for the comfort of Nick's soundproof limousine.

Ten

The next morning, I kneel before the vibrant painting of Goddess Lakshmi mounted on my bedroom wall. A graceful woman with golden skin, four hands, and a beatific smile, she wears a gold-embroidered red sari and stands on a blooming lotus flower. Her all-knowing eyes observe every moment of my life and of Ma's life too.

Ma prays to the Hindu deities in a private way, at an altar in her room, but she doesn't know that I talk to Lakshmi, or *mata*, the mother goddess of prosperity, wealth, purity, and generosity. I ask mata for inner strength, for a sense of purpose, and renewed energy infuses me.

At work, I'm grateful for this extra fortification when a deeply troubled woman wanders into the shop. She's wearing mauve lipstick, khaki slacks, and a black wool sweater, her sculpted features delicate and narrow.

"Are you looking for a sari?" I ask her.

Breaths of blue emptiness rush from her, revealing a new, half-empty bungalow, forlorn windows gazing in at her loneliness. Her past flits through the shadows—another house, bigger. A husband, a garden, friends on the patio.

"Are you Lakshmi?" she asks. Her eyes look familiar, the way she sighs when she gazes off to the left, the way her hair falls perfect and straight, like a wall.

"Do I know you?" I ask.

"My sister, Chelsea, owns the shop next door."

"Oh, you're Chelsea's sister! Lillian, right? How can I help you?"

"She said you would give me a good deal," she says in a voice as soft as lace. "I need curtains for my new house."

Curtains, of course. So the windows won't watch her with such pity. "I can help. You want sari fabric." In America, saris have many uses. I lead her to the reams of fabric on shelves by the counter. "We have all types of silk and cotton patterns. Most are mass produced in the mills, and some are custom woven."

"There are so many! I don't know which to choose. I hear you're really good at helping people find the right—"

"For you, maybe yellow roses, translucent, to let in the light."

She runs her fingers along the silk. "I love this. I think it will go well with my couch."

"Take a sample home, and if you like it, come back."

"I'll try, but I don't get a lot of time to myself." An image of a boy hurtles toward me. He's creamy skinned, his fine hair the color of sunset, his delicate features long and narrow. He might be eight years old, or younger. His frame is slight, vulnerable, like a sand sculpture. He builds an invisible wall around himself, a buffer to keep out blaring voices, blinding colors with jagged edges. Nothing will penetrate his ramparts, an army of imaginary soldiers protecting him. He sits cross-legged, rocking back and forth, and Lillian's insides squeeze with despair.

"What's his name?" I ask her.

Startled, she steps back. "Who?"

"Your son—what's his name? Chelsea told me you have a son."

Her face softens. "Jeremy. He's difficult, and . . . I've had a hard time getting through to him lately." Her mind closes, desperation extinguishing the image of the boy.

How can I help her? An odd feeling comes to me, as if an invisible hook is pulling me out of the store, to Lillian's house. "Let me come to your place," I say. "I'll bring some samples."

"Really, it's not necessary."

"I insist. I can measure your windows. I know someone who can sew the curtains for you."

"I don't know, I—"

"It will be no problem for me. Really."

"All right. How about next week?"

I nod and take down her address. As she leaves, I wonder what I'm getting myself into.

I spend the rest of the day working on Asha's account and gathering fabric samples for Lillian. Just after noon, Mitra's special Kathak costume arrives by UPS from the seamstress. It's exactly what I envisioned. I call Mitra, and she arrives just before closing. I take her into the office and unfold the costume for her. The yellow shimmers, the paisley pattern just as I pictured it.

Mitra's mouth opens in awe. "The costume—where did you get this pattern?" Tears slip down her cheeks. "This is exactly what I wore—"

"When you were little, on the beach, with your father."

"But a much smaller version. How did you know? Can you see such things so clearly?"

"It was fuzzy at first, but I had a feeling. The images, they just came to me."

"Oh, Lakshmi. But why?"

"Will you wear this to the dance performance? I know it will bring you good luck."

"How do you know? How can it possibly?" Her hope

spreads across the yellow Banarasi silk, sinking into the long choli shirt, slipping into the folds of the ghaghara, the flared skirt.

"Please trust me, Mitra. You have to invite your father. Will you promise? Before it's too late."

"Oh, Lakshmi." She bursts into tears and wraps me in a tight, desperate hug.

Eleven

*N*ear closing time, Nick and Asha show up at the shop with a woman who can only be Asha's sister. She has Asha's eyes, but her body is slim, and her beauty lies in her smooth movements as she adjusts the strap of her handbag over her shoulder. She's understated, dressed in jeans and a white blouse. Asha introduces her as Chitra, but the name dissolves and I'm aware only of Nick, who's decked out in a perfect black suit today. Now I know why Pooja thinks he's *cute*. A heavenly tailor must've measured every inch of muscle, and now the fabric drapes over his limbs in harmony with his stride. He gives me a slight, professional nod, the glint in his eye betraying our secret.

I barely register Asha in her navy blue sari, her face

made up, her luminous eyes rimmed with kohl. Enormous gold earrings dangle from her ears.

"We must clothe Chitra for the wedding," Asha announces. "Look at these jeans she's always wearing!"

A flash of *knowing* makes a last-ditch attempt to warn me. Ravi Ganguli appears like a watery mirage, handsome and polished. *Don't do it,* he says, and then the *knowing* spins away.

Don't do what?

"Nick, take me to the jewelry, will you?" Asha says in a theatrical voice. "I must have only the best gold. I'm having some family heirlooms brought from Mumbai, but I must have more bangles."

"Sanjay!" Ma screeches at Mr. Basu. "Show her only the good bangles, not the costume fashion jewelry you always show, nah?"

Mr. Basu reddens. "We have many fine bangles from Orissa," he tells Asha.

"Vijay will come one day soon," Asha says. "We must find a perfect kurta for him."

"Bring him anytime," Ma says, doing the sideways head nod.

Pooja waits on Chitra while Ma glides around, working the room. A strange buzzing fills my ears.

Nick glances at me and I quiver, inflating into a delicate balloon while he wheels Asha to the glass case of gold jewelry. "I meant to tell you, Bibu," Ma whispers in my ear.

"Ravi's parents called this morning, after you left." Her words blast me back to reality.

"That's lovely, Ma. What did they say?"

"They've consulted the astrologer, and the auspicious date for you and Ravi may fall sooner than six months from now! That is, if you and Ravi get on."

"That's wonderful, Ma!" a part of me says. Another part of me is watching Asha and Nick.

"I am so happy I can barely contain myself. This was all meant to happen. I have never been more hopeful in my life."

"Ma—" I take her warm hand, see the brightness of tears in her eyes, and my heart turns upside down.

Asha summons her sister to the saris.

This is my forte, finding saris, only the *knowing* has taken leave again. Then a boy walks in looking overwhelmed, wallet in hand. Ma motions to me to help him, to keep him out of Asha's hair. She hasn't closed the shop today.

The boy says his name is Anu. "I've been saving up for two years, but I have no idea what my mother will like for her birthday. She wants a sari. She keeps hinting! But when my sister buys her saris, she always hates them and yells." Beneath a map of acne, a handsome face is waiting to emerge.

"No problem, I can help you. It's always difficult for a boy to buy his first sari." I try to smile. I have to pretend I know what I'm doing.

"Thank you, Ms. Lakshmi—I've heard all about you. And I . . . have only two hundred dollars. I'm so worried. If my ma doesn't like a gift, we never hear the end of it. She even threw a sari out on the street last year! It was a gift from my sister. She cried."

"Oh, I'm so sorry!" Two hundred dollars limits his options, and I see no images to guide me. "Tell me more about your mother," I say, glancing at Nick. His back is to me, and Asha's poring over the jewelry.

"She's a software engineer," Anu says. "She likes to cook and play rummy, and she quit smoking three years ago. Now she swims at the local pool. She wears goggles. She has a temper . . ."

As he speaks, my fingers move along the shelves, resting on one sari, then another.

"Lakshmi, come and see which saris are best for Chitra!" Ma shouts.

"I'll be there soon, Ma!" I don't want the boy to spend all his hard-earned money. I choose an attractive midnight blue georgette sari. "Will this work for your mother, Anu?"

"It's so cool, Ms. Lakshmi. My mother likes blue."

"It's within your budget, and you'll have a little money left over." I'm not sure I'm giving him the perfect sari for his mother, but I've done my best. I ring him up and watch him leave, a bounce in his step.

Then I run over to Chitra, who stands nearly a head taller than Asha. "Horizontal stripes," I say. "Maybe silver and dark." *So Chitra won't look so tall.* No, no! I can't make decisions based on a woman's appearance. The *knowing* doesn't work that way, but there I am, pulling out saris with busy, striped patterns.

Nick is watching. The silent driver, always in the background.

Chitra frowns, her thin lips forming an upside-down half moon. Perhaps she needs translucent, slimming chiffon to make her resemble a fairy princess. My fingers touch the chiffon, then move to more stripes.

"Lakshmi, are you all right?" Ma asks.

"I'm fine, just trying to decide on the right pattern for the sister of the bride."

"Lakshmi's well known for her ability to predict which sari will bring good fortune," Asha tells her sister.

Chitra narrows her gaze. "A legend, are you? Like a fortune-teller?"

"Not exactly," I say.

"She has the eye," Ma says.

Not anymore. My fingers move from one fabric to another, my heart beating faster. The chiffon—ethereal. No, too lightweight. I grab the striped sari and hand it to Chitra, but already her eyes glitter with hostility. She gives Asha a triumphant look. "There, I told you this *Mystic Elegance* would charge you far too much for nothing. This Lakshmi can't read your mind. She has no idea—"

"I didn't say I could read minds," I say.

Nick gives me a curious look.

"She's nothing but a fraud," Chitra says. "Wants me to look exactly like a . . . zebra!" She holds up the sari in front of the mirror, and to my horror, I realize she's right. She would resemble a cross between a zebra and a giraffe in that sari. A dry lump rises in my throat. My limbs feel weak.

Ma leans against the counter, breathing shallowly. Asha taps a finger to her chin. Outside, a horn blares insistently.

Asha turns to Nick. "Is that your car alarm?"

"I'm on it." He's already heading out, and as the door closes behind him, images flood into me in a crazy zoo of color and sound. Asha's worrying that her fiancé won't return from India on time for the wedding. Ma has a sparkling secret up her sleeve, and Pooja wonders whether her wedding feast will be vegetarian. I freeze at the counter, my fingers curled into fists. Now I know for certain. Nick obscures the *knowing*. But how?

The insistent blare of the horn stops abruptly, and silence sneaks into the shop. I know how to help Chitra, but I don't have much time.

I grab the chiffon sari.

"I meant to pick this one," I say.

The shop holds its breath, not a molecule of fabric daring to move. I stuff the zebra sari onto the shelf, out of view.

Chitra holds the chiffon up in the mirror, and she's transformed into a mythical creature of beauty.

Asha breaks out in a delighted smile. "Absolutely perfect. We could never find a better sari!"

Twelve

Pooja and Mr. Basu rush over to help Chitra and Asha, while Ma drags me into the office. The *knowing* drapes around my shoulders away from Nick.

"What was that all about?" she whispers. "What is going on?"

"I must be catching a cold or something." I collapse into a chair. "I nearly lost Asha's business. I must be tired!"

"Now take your time, gather your wits. It's a good thing it's Friday. Maybe you need a weekend off, nah?"

"I'm taking Pooja to her wedding rehearsal on Sunday." I tell Ma about my secret plan to hire the limousine. "I'm getting an extra-good deal."

"Ah, the rehearsal. Yes, her parents invited me," Ma says.

"I hope you know what you're doing, Bibu. Make sure she gets there!" She bustles out into the store, and when I emerge from the office, the *knowing* spirals away.

Nick's back.

"And now, Lakshmi, you will measure Nick for a kurta!" Asha says.

"What? Who, me?"

"You're the best measurer we have." Ma slaps the tape measure into my hand.

"I want him in a respectable, yet elegant, kurta pajama," Asha says.

I glance at Ma. "I'm sure that Pooja can—"

"Certainly not!" Asha says. "Pooja says your hand is the most accurate for measuring."

Pooja's face falls with disappointment.

"But really, I'm not the best," I say.

"You are!" Ma says.

The tape measure resembles a foreign artifact. I'm sure I've forgotten how to use one.

Then Mr. Basu pushes me forward. I nearly stumble over Nick.

"Lakshmi will measure you in the dressing room," Mr. Basu says in a loud voice. Nick's already heading into the dressing room and there I am, packed in with him, surrounded by mirrors. An image of a blond god smiles back. He's more than a head taller than me.

He stares at me in the mirror.

I push the glasses up on my nose. My fingers tremble. I beg the gods to banish the blush in my cheeks. "I, uh, have to measure you."

"Put your magic hands to work."

"Could you take off your jacket? Just, um, hang your coat there on that hook."

"Do I need to take off my shirt?" He's flirting, the way Sean did. A flicker of memory prods at me. Sean coming to my cubicle at Overseas Investments, sweet-talking me, insinuating himself into my life.

"That won't be necessary. Just lift your arms like that."

I measure Nick's neck, his torso, put my arms around him to measure his waist. He lifts his arms, the whole time a slight smile on his face, as if this is all a mating dance.

"So what's this getup you're measuring me for?" His voice spreads through me like deep blue sugar.

"It's a traditional outfit, formal."

"Like a sari?"

"Not exactly. Saris are very complex, difficult to put on, and they're made differently in different parts of India. Worn differently, too."

"Show me how you do it. My sister's birthday party is next weekend. She likes ethnic dress."

I feel curiously breathless. Perhaps we need more air in the dressing rooms. "I can't show you," I whisper. "I'm working."

"Then come to the party and show my sister how to put on a sari. It'll be a surprise. Asha told me that you do that sometimes—go to parties to help women try on saris."

My insides flutter. "Well—I could do it. If you think she might like it. But this wouldn't be a date, you know. I'm going to India—"

"I know, no date. I'll pick you up, bring you home—"

"I can drive myself."

"I insist. I'll pick you up."

"Okay, I'll do it." I find I'm looking forward to riding in the limousine again. I nearly forgot. He's driving me and Pooja to her wedding rehearsal.

Thirteen

*S*unday afternoon, clouds saunter across a brilliant blue sky as Nick drives me to Pooja's place. Grateful for a day of winter sunshine, biplanes trail across the sky, couples walk their dogs, and boats emerge from hibernation to glide along Cedarlake, white sails billowing in the breeze.

I'm riding in the limo's backseat, and as usual, the *knowing* has taken leave. Pink bubbles pop from my skin. How delicate, how fragile these orbs look today, their translucent membranes quivering in the light.

But why do they hound me like the paparazzi?

I'll ignore them for the sake of surprising Pooja. When she sees the limo, she'll exclaim with delight. Her wide smile brightens my thoughts but disappears when a shivery pink sphere dangles from my nose. Annoyed, I swat it away.

As Nick drives around the lake, he keeps glancing in the rearview mirror, his eyes hidden behind dark sunglasses. Oh—I'm not wearing my glasses, and I let my hair down. I forgot how my natural look affects men. But even when I wore a frumpy outfit and ponytail, Nick flirted with me.

I meet his gaze for a long moment, and he smiles. I pretend to look out the window. The bubbles float all around me in a maddening jumble. Why am I affected this way? Why do I want Nick to take off the shades so I can see his eyes, so blue they make the world look drab?

He's decked out in a black suit to match his driver's cap. From my vantage in the backseat, his features are concrete, unreadable. He's strangely familiar, and yet we are as distant as continents. I must look foreign in my silver-blue pleated sari, gold bangles, and necklace. I bite my lip, a flutter of nervousness whisking through me.

I take a deep breath and try to relax. Everything had better go smoothly at the rehearsal. Pooja's family and friends will be waiting at the temple. I picture Dipak pacing, pockets of sweat dampening his armpits. Dipak and Pooja. They fit like two perfect pieces in a cosmic puzzle.

Everyone will cheer when she steps from the limo, her smile warming the crowd. On the way, we'll pour champagne from this small wine bar, lit from the inside with fluorescent pink bulbs.

The seats, smooth and shiny, look new, and a clean pine scent touches the air. The engine vibrates through me and I wonder what celebrity secrets have unfolded in here, what couples have consummated their marriages—

Don't go there.

Nick must've seen it all. He keeps all his limousine secrets tucked up under his cap.

"Thanks for agreeing to do this," I tell him. I run my hands along the smooth vinyl seat. "I can hardly wait to see Pooja's face. She has a bit of a crush on you, but don't tell her I told you that. She's getting married."

"Which one is Pooja again?" He glances at me in the rearview mirror.

"You don't remember her? The pretty young thing with the frizzy hair? Really slim? Don't flirt with her, though. She's engaged."

"Oh, her. She's a nice kid. Now, if you had a crush on me . . ."

I let out a tiny, nervous laugh. "Why would I—I mean, why would you care?" Am I flirting? Playing coy with this driver? What has come over me?

"All I'm saying is I would pay attention." He turns away from the lake, the limo climbing along a narrow street lined with ornamental pear trees and pastel bungalows.

"Oh. I see." A creeping heat travels from my cheeks to my ears. I make a point of wiping the condensation on the window. Why can't I think of a better comeback?

Nick clears his throat. "Is she going to one of those arranged marriages?" His voice slides across the seat and rests on my shoulders.

"Semi-arranged."

"Does she love the guy?"

"If she doesn't now, she will."

"Hell of a way to go." He turns up the radio a half degree. A Billie Holiday melody, "My Old Flame," slinks from the speakers.

"You make it sound like she's getting killed. She's completely excited." I arrange my sari, which suddenly goes tight around my thighs. "If you met Dipak, you'd like him."

"How well does she know him?"

"Since they were children. She wants to marry him, and everyone's very happy for her. We're celebrating. You sure you know the way?" I lean forward so he can hear me, and I catch a whiff of his metallic aftershave.

"Trust me. I always know the way."

I sit back, feeling oddly comforted.

He does know exactly where to find Pooja's place, a modern green apartment building sandwiched between two others. A few scrawny magnolia trees struggle up in the bathroom-size yards, where the sod has been hastily unrolled between stretches of concrete. There's a faint odor of sulfur in the air, as if a septic tank is leaking somewhere. Traffic noise foams up in the distance.

Nick parks in the guest lot, and in a second he's opening my door. My arm brushes his as I hold up my sari and walk to the front door. I ring the bell for Pooja's apartment and wait. And wait.

Nick's standing next to the limo, hands in his pants pockets. He never taps a foot or glances at his watch. A good quality in a driver. Patience.

I have only a thimble of patience.

Finally, thumping footsteps come down the stairs and Pooja opens the door. I suck in a breath.

She's a kleptomaniac's dream. In her shiny, red silk sari, gold jewels, and precious gems, she's a gleaming vision with frizzy hair. A jewelry shop hung its entire inventory from her limbs. And yet beneath the fancy garb, she's a delicate dewdrop.

"Oh, Lakshmi," she whispers, "you look lovely." Her voice trembles. Intricate patterns of henna cover her hands and climb across her forehead.

"No, you're the lovely one, Pooja! You're an absolute . . . you're beautiful." I give her a hug, as best I can with all the metal and stones in the way. Her body shakes a bit, and her skin is warmer than usual.

"Do you think so?" She glances past me at the limousine, at Nick standing there like a broad-shouldered statue, and she covers her mouth. "What have you done, Lakshmi? Oh, you got a limo for me. Are you serious? Why did you go and do that?" She's grinning, pinpoints of color springing up in her cheeks.

"For you—so we can arrive in style." I take her arm.

"Ma and Baba will be there! Oh, I can't wait to show them!"

"Are you ready?"

"Oh, you shouldn't have done it, shouldn't have." Her eyes are watery. She slings her handbag over her shoulder and takes my hand in a tight grip. Her fingers are cool. "Let's go, Lakshmi. I have to get out of here." She takes a deep breath, and I take her to the car.

Nick opens the door for us, and Pooja assesses him before getting into the backseat. "He's a cutie," she whispers to me, a hint of longing in her voice. I put a finger to my lips, hoping that Nick didn't hear.

He pulls out easily and threads back through town toward the highway.

"Do you know where the temple is?" I ask.

"I know the way everywhere," Nick says.

Arrogant, I'm thinking as I sit back.

"Oh, Lakshmi—I haven't slept a wink and my armpits are itching," Pooja says. Her fingers are slender tendrils clinging to the armrest.

"I'm sure all brides go through this. You'll be fine. It's only a rehearsal."

Her black eyes implore me. "Are you certain? Do you see it? I mean, my future? Do you see Dipak and me happy together? Is that the kind of thing you can see?"

Nick glances in the mirror, his brows furrowing.

I nod and lie, because at the moment, I see nothing but bubbles. "You're blissful, sitting at a bay window with lovely views, and you'll have the most beautiful children." I see nothing but the backseat and the triangle of road ahead.

Pooja lets go of my hand, fumbles in her purse, and produces a miniature bottle with a Glenlivet label. Whisky! But Pooja doesn't drink. A mere sip of wine makes her tipsy. "I need to calm my nerves," she says and takes a swig.

"Pooja! You can't drink before your rehearsal," I whisper.

"Just a shot to fortify me." Her cheeks are flushed.

"You okay back there?" Nick glances in the mirror again.

"I'm not feeling well, so nervous." Pooja takes another gulp of whisky. "Is this normal, Lakshmi? Tell me."

Nick glances in the mirror again.

"This will be your second happiest day," I say. "I'm here for you. Hang in there. Once the ceremony begins, it'll be just like riding a bike."

She gives me a pleading look. "Are you sure? You've never been married, have you?"

"No, but I've helped many through the pre-wedding jitters."

"I can stop the car if you want to get out," Nick says. "There's a rest area in a few miles."

"I need more whisky." Pooja stares forlornly at the nearly empty bottle.

I snatch the bottle from her. "You need fresh air."

At the rest area, Nick helps Pooja out of the car. She takes a deep breath. "Okay, I'll get some coffee then." She totters away toward the coffee stand near the restrooms, the wind whipping her hair and jingling her bangles. She's a walking jewelry store, drawing stares from passing truckers and travelers.

I stand awkwardly next to the limo, the sari pressed against my legs. The closer I get to Nick, the more the bubble bath fizzes around me.

"We have to get her straightened out before we reach the temple," I say.

"Maybe she's not ready," he says.

I give him a sharp look. "Not ready for what?"

"To get married."

"Of course she is. She has the jitters, that's all."

"It's more than jitters. She's physically ill."

"She'll be fine. It's a big deal having all the family there waiting." I set my jaw.

"Why does she have to stick to your traditions?"

"They're not my traditions," I say, and I realize that these half-arranged marriages feel alien to me as well. "They belong to our ancestors, to our culture."

"You don't seem so traditional."

I glance toward Pooja, who is waiting in the coffee line, her arms crossed over her chest. She looks so forlorn and fragile that I want to grab her before the wind carries her away.

"Okay, I'm not traditional. I grew up here. I'm an American," I say. "So is Pooja. But she's always been very close to her parents. They've always expected her to marry."

"That doesn't mean she should do it."

"Haven't you heard of American brides getting nervous? Where do you think the term 'cold feet' comes from?"

"She has more than cold feet. She's a walking ice block."

"She's a grown-up. Besides, she loves Dipak."

"How do you recognize true love?"

"You have to see the two of them together. Then you would know! Why are you intruding, anyway? I hired you to drive me and Pooja to the rehearsal, not to break up her marriage!"

Nick holds up his hands, palms forward. "Whoa—look, I hate to see someone get pushed into a marriage she doesn't really want just to satisfy some family tradition. Love is the one thing in life that should not be compromised."

"Compromised! You think Pooja is compromising?" I'm

seething now, but I muster my best smile as Pooja returns, sipping coffee. She looks marginally refreshed.

We're going to be twenty minutes late, not that time would matter so much in India, but it matters here, and the freeway's slowly clogging with traffic.

I lean back in the car, my fingers curling into fists. Please, let this day go smoothly.

Pooja finishes her coffee, then gives me a woozy look. Her cheeks are pale. I touch her forehead. Her skin feels cool and damp.

"Pooja, what is it?"

"I took a sedative, a pill for anxiety, before—"

"Before what? Before the whisky?"

She nods. She's turning into a regular addict overnight.

"You should never mix alcohol and drugs!" I shout.

Nick frowns into the mirror. "Everything okay?"

"I'm so sorry, Lakshmi," Pooja whispers. "It's just that, you know, Dipak doesn't understand how much I want to be a doctor. And I love San Francisco."

"I'll turn around," Nick says. "Take you home."

"No, you won't!" I shout. "Just because she took a pill doesn't mean she's calling off the wedding. She's not giving up so easily, are you, Pooja?"

"Dipak wants to stay near his parents," Pooja goes on. "I want to go to California. Oh, I don't know . . ." Her voice trails off.

"You don't know?" I say incredulously. "Look, we'll deliver you to your family, and you can talk to your parents, to Dipak." *Make sure she gets there,* Ma said.

"They won't understand. I don't want to go."

"She doesn't want to go," Nick says.

"Nick!" I shout. "Look, Pooja. I didn't realize you were so . . . worried about all this. Drink some water, and all will be well."

"There's water in the pocket behind the seat," Nick says. "To your left."

The spring water calms Pooja for now.

"Drive faster, Nick," I say. "We have to get to the temple. She'll feel better with her family."

Nick exits the freeway in Bellevue and heads uptown. My shoulders relax. I half believed he wouldn't take Pooja to the temple. "Talk to Dipak," I tell her.

Pooja presses the back of her hand to her forehead.

Nick pulls up to the curb in front of the Hindu temple, a modern construction with vaulted ceilings and cedar siding. If it weren't for the colorful, stained-glass windows depicting Hindu deities, you would hardly know it was a temple.

A group of well-dressed family members congregates on the steps. Pooja slides down in the seat, grips the armrest. "I can't face Dipak. I can't—"

"Come on, Pooja. Promise you'll talk to him about

going to San Francisco. Let him know how important this is to you, please!" I tell her. I am annoyed. We are so late! I don't want to go out there, don't want to fall into this impending disaster.

"Okay, I have nothing to lose." She sucks in a deep breath, exhales through her nose.

Nick rushes around to open her door, and she steps out, a glittering vision in the sunlight.

Immediately, the gaggle of relatives flies down the steps to gather around her. *Where have you been? You look beautiful. You came in a limo!*

The crowd parts, falls into a hush, and there's Dipak, broad-shouldered and regal in his off-white kurta pajama threaded with gold, his wavy hair oiled back. He descends the steps, his square jaw firm, and I hold my breath, not daring to hope. He and Pooja gaze at each other for a long moment, and a sparkle of possibility hovers between them. Then he scoops Pooja into his arms and carries her up the steps, across the threshold and into the temple.

Fourteen

"She'll be okay, and I don't want to go in there," I say. I am too aggravated.

"Look, I'm sorry I made you late for the rehearsal," Nick says.

"Oh, it wasn't your fault. Pooja just needed a little cajoling."

"I can take you home if you want. Or I can drive to Port Gamble, out on the peninsula. Great view of the Hood Canal. You can see right across the water. Ever been there?"

"I don't get away from the shop too much these days."

"There's a lot to see here, Lakshmi."

"Fine. Let's go then." What do I have to lose? I sit back, glad for the soft lullaby of the car engine as Nick drives back over the Tacoma Narrows Bridge and up past Gig Harbor along the Olympic Peninsula, fir and pine trees rising dense on both sides of the highway. We're heading farther from the city, away from the noise. I'm grateful for the quiet expanse of road and the jagged mountain peaks rising in the west. The slanting winter sunlight stretches down to the southwest, lending an orange-yellow hue to the dimming sky.

Nick takes off his sunglasses. How can such a stubborn, annoying man have eyes of such soft, caring blue?

Soon the road narrows, and the occasional neighborhoods give way to quaint farmhouses surrounded by meadows and thickets. The road curves around past a park. A wooden sign reads Welcome to Port Gamble and ends in a tiny New England–style town of manicured lawns, turn-of-the-century mansions, and, only a block to the west, the glinting ocean.

Nick parks on the main street, Rainier Avenue, lined with towering maples and elms. We've driven back in time, unrolling the years to the late 1800s.

A spark of enthusiasm flares inside me. How long has it been since I've driven somewhere new on a whim? "This is a storybook town!" I exclaim. "There's a spa, and didn't we pass a bookstore in that red house? Dauntless Bookstore? A museum! And a general store."

"This was an old mill town, still operating until a

decade ago," Nick says. "None of these historic homes can be upgraded—they're landmarks. My parents live near here, in Port Westwood. I grew up there. Maybe I'll show you sometime." He takes off his jacket and hands it to me across the seat. "Here, put this on. It's chilly out there."

Around my shoulders, his jacket feels heavy and warm as we stroll along the sidewalk. "I didn't expect to be out here today," I say.

"Sometimes things don't go according to plan," Nick says.

"Yeah, right. Are you charging me extra for this side trip?"

"It's on me." Nick follows me into a fragrant boutique called the Rugosa Rose. He's right next to me as I sniff soaps and thumb through greeting cards, the wooden floor creaking beneath our feet. The bubbles burst out of me and float around the store.

"You're like my sister," he says. "You both like soap."

"We have a wedding package special," the girl behind the counter says. "Got everything you need from lotions to massage oils." Half her hair is pink, half black, and she's wearing a scarf around her waist, over tight jeans and T-shirt.

"Thanks, but there's no wedding going on here," I say.

"Massage oil sounds like fun." Nick picks up the package in question, gives me a wink.

I stomp out, my ears ablaze. "What was that about?"

"Have a little fun, Lakshmi." He takes my hand. "When was the last time you enjoyed your day without work?" His fingers are warm and firm, his hand big and comforting.

My throat goes dry. He's right. The needs of others clamor at me like babies, always crying for nurturing. And now, I feel the clean air moving through me, nourishing me, and the *knowing* lies dormant, giving me a break.

"Come on, I want to show you something." He leads me up a grassy slope to an ancient cemetery, some of the marble headstones so old that the names and dates have worn off. On the hilltop, the wind is strong and smells of freshly cut grass, and the Pacific Ocean rushes away in stutters of white-capped waves. There's a crazy openness here, a feeling that I could lift off and drift away.

"Buena Vista Cemetery," Nick says. "Dates from the mid-1800s. First U.S. Navy Coxswain Gustave Englebrecht of the USS *Massachusetts* died in a skirmish with Haida raiders."

"Wow, you remember all that?"

"I've been here a million times. Come up here to think. Englebrecht was the first U.S. Navy man killed in the Pacific."

He shows me a burial plot surrounded by an iron fence, but without a headstone. "That's where the town founder, Josiah Keller, is buried. Died in the 1860s, I think."

My teeth are chattering now, but Nick's hand still feels warm. I don't want to let go. How silly is that? "This feels like the town that time forgot," I say. I close my eyes and take in the rush of the wind, the distant voices of tourists sauntering through the graveyard, and I realize that there's a bizarre peace in standing among the dead. The dead don't have needs, their thoughts don't assault me, and at this moment, Nick is the only buffer between me and the living.

"The Klallam people used to live here," he says. "Until the mills came. I feel their ghosts here."

"What happened to them?"

"They were asked to move. There was a treaty, but it wasn't entirely fair to the Klallam people. The usual story of the white man taking over." He's still holding my hand as if it's the most natural thing to do, although I barely know him.

Maybe he won't be like Sean, who sometimes wouldn't hold my hand in public, around people who knew his family. He never would've taken me to a cemetery to talk about the way the native people were treated. Never would've rallied to the defense of a confused girl like Pooja, either.

"Come on—let's go. Your lips are blue," Nick says.

Sean wouldn't have cared if I was cold. He would've told me to slap on more lipstick.

When we get back to the car, I find I don't want to leave just yet. "What about that tearoom across the street? Why don't we get a coffee?"

"Are you allowed to fraternize with the help?" Nick gives me another half smile, and I'm blushing but hoping he can't tell in this wind.

The tea room is small, intimate, and noisy, and we're squished at a round corner table near a glass case full of cinnamon rolls and scones. "The smell in here—it's heavenly," I say.

"Reminds me of my mother's baking," Nick says.

The warm air thaws me while outside the wind whips up to a screech.

"So tell me about your guy in India," Nick says over coffee. "Is this an arranged deal too?"

I look at Nick, at the rugged lines of his profile, the strong jaw. "Arranged marriages have been working in India for generations."

"And young brides get burned and disfigured if they don't pay enough dowry money to the man's family," he says. "I read about this stuff in the papers."

The foam bubbles make a renewed appearance. I become hyperaware of Nick's body beside me, the scent of his aftershave and an underlying masculine smell. A curious fluttering begins in the center of my belly.

"Bride burning still happens," I say. "But not everywhere, and not in enlightened families."

"This guy in India—is he enlightened then?"

"All I know is that he comes from a good family, has a

good job, and he's Bengali. He speaks my mother's language—"

"What about your language, Lakshmi? Why does your mother's language matter so much?"

"I suppose we are traditional in that way. Ma's been waiting to tell our extended family that I've finally found the right guy. They keep pestering her about having an unmarried daughter."

"Families don't know everything," he says. "Neither do mothers."

"Mine do!"

His laughter has a bitter edge. "Wake up, there's a world out there, and you gotta live in it. Not with your whole family."

"Family is the most important thing in the world," I say, and that's when the room goes dark. The whir of the coffee machine stops abruptly, there's a popping sound in a back room, and somebody says, "Oh, shit."

"What's going on?" I say, then notice that although the sun is setting, there are no lights anywhere on the street.

"The power's out!" a woman says.

People are talking excitedly and in that instant, Nick moves close to me and his lips brush mine in the darkness. Or am I imagining things? I'm mesmerized, points of crazy electricity buzzing in my mind, short-circuiting every thread of thought. I can't see a thing, and then Nick is lifting me to my feet, his arms on mine, taking my elbow. The smell of him is so close, the scent of his aftershave and an underlying scent all his own, a mixture of soap and ever-green.

"Come on, let's get out of here." His hand is on my waist as he steers me to the door and then back to the car.

Fifteen

Monday morning at the shop, I can't dispel the feeling of Nick's lips brushing mine. On the way home from Port Gamble, we chatted about superficial subjects, while the kiss hovered like a secret balloon between us. And what of Pooja? Ma said that she went through with the wedding rehearsal but wept while repeating her vows.

Today Pooja arrives at work in cotton shirt and jeans, surrounded by quiet contemplation. I want to ask all sorts of questions, and I finally corner her in the office as she's coming out of the bathroom. "So spill, Pooja. What's up?"

"I've been accepted to the University in San Francisco. I'm going."

"Pooja, that's fabulous. But what about Dipak?"

"We discussed everything—and oh, Lakshmi, he must really love me." She breaks into a smile. "He's going to join me when he finishes his studies here. We'll be apart for only a few months."

I rest my hands on her shoulders. "I knew all would work out for the best." A soft cloud of promise floats up from her.

"What about you, Lakshmi? You went off with that cute driver—what did you two do? Did you, you know—"

"Pooja, it was nothing like that. I agreed to go to Nick's sister's birthday party Saturday night. I promised to help her try on saris."

"Oh, you'll have fun. He's picking you up?"

I nod, dismissing my interlude with him as temporary insanity. This Saturday will be a job, all business. But the week shuffles by so slowly. Asha does not return, but she yells orders over the phone, keeping us busy. Ma prepares for her weekend playing bridge with her good friend, Sonia, in Kent. We'll close the shop early Saturday, and she'll spend the night at Sonia's and return Sunday.

My Thursday lunch with Nisha and Mitra takes forever to arrive. Nisha's in a soft black suit, her hair done up in a bun.

Decked out in a loud orange sweater and a tight black skirt, Mitra chews her salad with gusto. "Are you ready to meet Mr. Ravi?" she asks me.

"As ready as I'll ever be." I think of the brief messages I've traded with Ravi Ganguli all week. I'm getting to know him from a distance, email by email, photo by photo. He already feels like a friend.

"How's the big Bollywood wedding coming along?" Nisha asks.

I stir my lemonade with a straw. "Asha's demanding. I got to see her on the set. She wasn't actually filming. They do a lot of waiting around, preparing the set, and there are way more people involved than I ever imagined."

"I read in *Star* magazine that her marriage to Vijay was arranged," Nisha said. "They're deeply in love. She expounds upon the virtues of arranged marriages. See, they do work. Mine worked, and Asha's happy. So I hope you're not getting cold feet."

"I don't have cold feet!" I say. "Besides, Ravi and I haven't actually met. I haven't decided."

Mitra pats my arm, her eyes shining with hope. "Lakshmi, I have to thank you. I took your advice and went to see my parents. It was really hard to talk to my father, but I was glad I went. He looked so fragile." Her voice breaks, and I catch a glimpse of her father, who is made of wrinkled skin and bone in a white dhoti punjabi, the pants gently flaring at the ankles, his feet clad in brown chappals. After twenty-five years in America, he still looks as if he's just stepped off the plane from India and hasn't had time to iron his shirt.

"I'm proud of you, Mitra," I say.

"I invited them to my dance performance," she says. "My father said nothing, but my mother said she would try to convince him to come. There's something in that costume you gave me, a magic that gave me strength to face him again, even if he disapproves of me. I don't know how much longer he has, and, well . . ." She gazes into her olives and onions.

"He missed you, even if he doesn't show it." I take a bite of my veggie sandwich.

"I wish I could see my father more often," Nisha says, moving the stir-fried vegetables around on her plate. "I miss my parents terribly. They may come for a visit soon, when the weather gets hot in Delhi."

I see her running through the alley again, stopping at an apartment building and glancing up at a light in a window. Is this a memory of childhood? Was she playing a game? Hide-and-seek?

"How's Rakesh?" I ask her. "What about your trip to Baja?"

"He's on a business trip in San Diego. We postponed Baja to next month, maybe."

"He'll postpone forever if you don't pin him down," Mitra says. "Tell him you'll get a divorce—"

"He's a wonderful husband!" Nisha says. "I can't imagine even considering a divorce. He gives me everything I ask for. He even cooks for me when he's home, does the laundry, takes me out for dinner. He's just terribly busy and I'm lonely. He's so ambitious. I want him around more often. He's a workaholic, always has been."

"Then tell him," Mitra says. "Tell him you need him at home."

A watery image flows toward me. Nisha's climbing the steps of the apartment building, her knuckles white as they grip the railing. Then the image vanishes, her mind locking itself away.

Sixteen

Thursday evening, when I email Nisha about a sari she ordered, I get an automated reply saying she's gone for three days. Did she finally get Rakesh to go to Baja?

Friday slides by in slow motion, and late Saturday morning, Ma leaves the shop early for Sonia's house in Kent. I have the jitters, knowing that Nick will soon arrive to take me to his sister's party.

Pooja and I close the shop around noon. I quickly let my hair down, remove my glasses, and apply a thin layer of pink lipstick. I put on a soft, mauve sari and gather up a few other saris, petticoats, and cholis to take with me. "Take the organza saris," Pooja says. She's the only other person left in the store. "Women always like those."

She strides to the front door, ready to lock up. Then she

freezes, backs up. "Holy smokes," she whispers. "Is that him? He looks different. He looks—oh my."

She's right. It's Nick, nearly at the door. He's in jeans, black boots, an open jacket, and a sweater, the rough lines of his face shadowed beneath the streetlights. There's something about him—a suggestion of all the things I long to reach.

A lump of sheer terror—and a great thrill—rises in my throat. My lips tingle with the memory of the phantom kiss in the darkness.

Pooja opens the door, converses with him in a hushed tone. I give her a *don't leave* look, but she's already waving at me, out the door and disappearing.

Nick's piercing blue eyes cut laser swaths through me. As he strides over, the kameezes blush and gather for whispered conversations. I imagine the saris slipping off the rack to wrap around his feet.

He takes my hand, my fingers lost in his. "Hey, Lakshmi," he says then lets go of my hand, but his gaze doesn't waver. "You look beautiful. That's a . . . silk sari you're wearing, right?"

"You got it right. Thanks." A soft heat spreads across my cheeks.

"Amazing. Is that just one piece or many?"

"It's a long stretch of unstitched fabric, like this." I take a silver silk sari off the shelf. "Indians believe that unstitched fabric is the most pure. Untouched."

"I like pure, untouched." Nick gives me a look, runs his fingers along the cloth. "So soft, like a woman's skin."

My breathing becomes shallow. "The story goes, the sari was born on the loom of a master weaver, who dreamed of women, of their shimmering tears, the drape of their hair, the rainbow colors of their many moods, their soft touch. And he kept weaving yards and yards of fabric—"

"So the sari *is* a woman." Nick picks up the silk and runs it through his fingers, stopping to capture the endpiece.

"Yes, I suppose. And when he'd finished he kept smiling. The weaver had created a pure woven fabric that embodied every aspect of the feminine."

Nick's watching me, his gaze traveling down to my bare navel above the sari hem.

"Look, we should leave now." I stride around, turning out the lights. "I have to set the alarm on the front door. We can go out the back way. I just need to use the restroom." I rush to take a few minutes in the restroom, to catch my breath and my bearings. Okay, this will be a business evening, an outing to help Nick's sister. So why am I breaking out in a sweat, and why are the invisible bubbles sprouting around my head?

When I come out, he's waiting in the hall. Just then, the doorknob jiggles. I hear a set of keys drop to the pavement, a muttered curse, someone picking up the keys.

"Someone's coming," I whisper. "Maybe they forgot something."

Ma, Mr. Basu, Pooja, and I are the only people who have keys. I yank Nick's sleeve and pull him back into the office, into the closet with the coats. If Ma is here, I don't want her to find me alone with the American driver. She's traditional in that way. She won't understand, even if I try to explain. I shut the closet door, leaving only a sliver-sized opening.

My heart pounds. I try to keep the sari from rustling. Nick's so close, I can feel the firm muscle of his arm, his pulse, the heat through his shirt.

The back door opens, shuts. Cold air wafts in. Footsteps in the hall! Breathing.

Through the opening in the closet, I see Ma rush into the office, bend to pick up her black handbag from her chair. A cloud of sandalwood scent drifts into my nose. Ma never uses perfume!

"Ah, thank the gods, it was here," she says. "I thought I'd lost it! Where was my head? We can't go to Vancouver without my passport!" Ma, going to Vancouver?

"*Thanda lege jabey,*" an affectionate voice says in Bengali.

Mr. Basu walks in, all dressed up in a suit, his two hairs slicked back. Mr. Basu!

"Oh, Sanjay!" Ma says. She and Mr. Basu step out into

the hall, out of view, their shadows falling across the office carpet. I try to keep my breathing silent, but the blood rushes in my ears. Nick is still holding my hand. What are Ma and Mr. Basu doing together? Ma's supposed to be with Sonia in Kent!

Then the shadows blend together, and the smack of lips colliding in a noisy kiss. Mr. Basu moans, and Ma makes a funny strangled sound.

Oh, no. Ma!

"Oh, Sanjay!" Ma says again in a husky voice, and I hear clattering as something gets knocked over. They back up into the bathroom, and a bottle falls from the sink and lands with a thump.

My heart races. The bathroom door slams, the giggling muffled inside. Ma screeches with laughter.

I push open the closet. "We have to get out of here!" I whisper.

Nick and I tiptoe down the hall and out the back door.

Seventeen

Nick brought a black BMW, not a limousine. I sit on a few CDs on the seat, maybe a box of tissues. There are hints of citrus and his metallic aftershave in the air. Ma's perfume still lingers in my nose.

Nick has his seat pushed all the way back to accommodate his legs. Long fingers curl over the steering wheel.

I arrange the sari around me, pull the pallu tightly over my bare shoulders. I wish I'd brought a sweater.

"I can't believe it," I say. "Ma and Mr. Basu!"

"What's wrong with the man? He seems cool to me."

"But she hates him! She always yells at him." And he's round!

"A sign of true love."

"Why didn't she tell me? Or anyone? Why didn't I see this coming? The golden bubbles," I say half to myself. "The yellow roses."

"Bubbles and roses? Is this Valentine's Day?" He turns the car onto Main Street, past closed shops and the town hall.

"I see them sometimes, I mean, thoughts coming out in bubbles and roses and things. You must think I'm crazy."

"I like crazy women."

Nick makes a smooth turn onto the waterfront road. The sky is a cloudless blue above us.

"I see what's important, what I need to see to make a difference—I feel so betrayed! I mean, how could she—"

"Enjoy her life?"

"No, no—that's not what I mean at all. How could she sneak around? Mr. Basu is taking advantage of her."

"She's a grown-up. She's your mother, so you can't imagine her having a life of her own, eh? I nearly hurled when I saw my mother in the nude master gardener calendar."

"What's that?"

"To raise funds for the county master gardeners, some of the members volunteer to be photographed nude in their gardens. It's all tasteful—flowers strategically placed, but it's really weird seeing your own mother that way. She's a good-looking woman, mind you, but a son doesn't want to see that. She posed behind her rusty wheelbarrow."

I can't help laughing. "Your mom sounds like a lively character!"

"So does yours, Lakshmi."

"Yes, but she's lonely and vulnerable. My father was her only true love. Mr. Basu sees she's lonely, and he pounced!"

"I wouldn't jump to conclusions. Maybe she enjoys his company. Like you're enjoying mine?" He raises an eyebrow at me.

I cross my arms over my chest. "Okay, I see your point."

"So what did that mean, what Mr. Basu said to your mother? At the store. Was that Bengali?"

"Oh—" I make a sour face. I'm not sure I want to remember. "*Thanda lege jabey.* It means, 'Careful, you'll catch cold.' Bengalis are known for wrapping themselves up at the slightest sign of cold. You might see a Bengali child wrapped in linen and wool, even on a warm summer day. It's what Bengalis are most afraid of, catching cold. Even though they love to vacation in the mountains. Speaking of catching cold, would you mind stopping by my house so I can get a sweater?"

"Sure thing."

When Nick steps into our house, the laws of physics change, altered by his breath. The strange heat between us dissipates in the ghostlike presence of my mother.

"Cool place. Homey." He follows me into the living room.

"Please, sit down." Suddenly I feel like a formal hostess.

He sits on the couch, and Shiva promptly appears and

settles in his lap. Nick strokes his fur and whispers to him in a secret language.

"He never does that," I say. "He never goes to a stranger like that."

"Animals like me." He winks at me, and I blush.

"I'll be right back." I rush off to my room, and when I return with a sweater, Nick's scratching Shiva behind the ears. "What's his name?"

"Shiva. The girl is Parvati, Shiva's consort in Hinduism. They're eternal . . . lovers. But Parvati's a bit shyer. She likes to hide."

"Let's find her." Nick puts Shiva gently on the floor and goes straight to the cabinet above the fridge, opens it, and there's Parvati, blinking out at us. She lets out a plaintive meow and Nick brings her out, cradling her as he carries her to the floor.

"How did you know she would be up there?" I ask.

"I had a cat who hid in cabinets all the time," he says. "Name was Charlie from *Charlie and the Chocolate Factory.*"

My heart warms. "Um, we should go, or we'll be late, won't we?"

The strange bubbles are bouncing around me again. But what the heck? Ma is out with Mr. Basu. What do I have to lose?

Nick comes to life behind the wheel as he drives to his parents' home in Port Westwood where the party is taking place, his eyes bright, his voice animated, as if his favorite place is the journey between two points. I could sit in the car beside him all day and night. He vibrates hot in my nerve endings.

Like a fever.

Yet riding next to him I feel safe, as if I could close my eyes and jump off the top of the Taj Mahal and land unharmed.

I lean back against the headrest and watch the hills and valleys speed by.

He turns off the highway abruptly onto a narrow road, past a green sign reading Port Westwood. "We're in the rain shadow of the Olympic Mountains here," he says. "During harvest, you can smell the lavender everywhere."

"Sounds lovely," I say dreamily.

"We don't get as much rain as other parts of the state. Lots of evergreens."

He slows in a small strip of quaint businesses—a library, brick town hall, community center, drugstore, ice cream shop, bakery. He turns down a dirt road lined with large oaks, cedars, and firs until we reach a clearing, and there, like a mirage against a backdrop of sky and sea, stands a blue Victorian with several cars in the driveway. Coiffed hedges and dormant flowerbeds stretch away into a forest of thick fir and pine and Western red cedar, and beyond the forest, the ocean twinkles. A misty peacefulness rises from the dewdrops gleaming in the grass.

"I went to Juan de Fuca High School down the street," Nick says, "played football, drove to the local drive-in more than once."

I try not to imagine Nick making out in a car with the prom queen. I glance at the garage, painted blue with white trim, set away from the house. Even the garage is surrounded by vines and lush vegetation.

On the porch, there's a swinging rattan bench with sagging pillows, and I imagine him sitting out here, gazing at passing freighters and ferries. I close my eyes and take in the silence—how wonderful it is not to have invisible lives crowding my head.

Inside, the scents of lavender and apple rise gently in the air. The ceilings dome in spacious arcs, and the house is furnished in dark, polished woods with sleek lines and soft touches—blankets draped over the backs of chairs and pillows on the couches. Laughter drifts from the kitchen, and two men are watching a football game in another room.

"Yo, bro!" Nick yells, leading me into the living room. One man stands, grabs Nick's hand, and they exchange a high-five greeting.

"Yo, Nick!" the man replies. Except for his stocky build and prominent nose, the man resembles Nick. He's holding a Heineken bottle in one hand, and he's dressed in a checkered flannel shirt and baggy jeans.

"When did you get here?" Nick asks.

"Couple of hours ago. This is my friend Hardy. He's staying here too. Partner at the firm."

Hardy is a dark-haired, thin man with a mustache, also in jeans and a T-shirt. He and Nick exchange greetings, and Hardy gives me a nod.

"Laurel stayed home tonight," Nick's brother says. "Holly picked up a cold in preschool."

Laurel and Holly?

"This is my brother Mike," Nick says. "He's an attorney. Mike, this is Lakshmi. She's got the sari shop—"

"Oh, you're Lakshmi!" Mike's eyes widen, and he shakes my hand in a firm grip. "Nick's told me all about you."

I smile. "What could he have told you?"

"How beautiful you are, for one thing," Mike says. "You weren't kidding, bro. Welcome to our crazy family, Lakshmi. We're only a little crazy. We're actually normal in real life."

I glance at Nick. He looks a bit embarrassed. "Yeah, we can be crazy," he says. "We like to play games. But it's a good kind of crazy."

"So what's up with the business?" Mike says. "Jerry's in the kitchen, wants to talk—"

"I'm about to go in there," Nick says. "This way, Lakshmi." He's holding my hand again, leading me down a hall. "Laurel's his wife and Holly's his two-year-old daughter."

I nod, my hands clammy. In the kitchen, everyone turns to us and smiles. The counters are covered with baskets of fruit and garlic and plates of cookies. My house—my mother's house—isn't as generous. Ma keeps the counters spotless, and even with all the spice and the scents of India, there's a kind of closed-in sterility. Ma likes to keep everything clean, keep her secrets hidden.

"Hey, Nick!" a tall man shouts. He's wearing a World's Worst Cook apron and embraces Nick in a bear hug, pats his back. I think of the way my relatives embrace, in a fluid, soft style. They're always dressed up for these occasions. But in Nick's house, family members crash into each other, and they're all wearing whatever they want, as if they closed their eyes, reached into their closets, and threw on whatever they touched.

This man with the apron is clearly Nick's brother. He's Nick but slimmer and narrower, as if he stood between two walls that squished him.

"Lakshmi!" he shouts and gives me the same bear hug. I'm squashed and momentarily unable to breathe.

"This is Jerry," Nick says.

"I know who you are. Nick described you—long hair, exotic." Jerry grins. "I'm so glad you could make it."

"So am I." Nick described me?

His mother embraces me as well, and I'm enveloped in the scents of perfume and bread and her own mother-smell.

141

She's a slim, regal woman with flushed cheeks, grayish-blond hair sticking to her sweaty forehead. Her eyes are shockingly light gray, as if the sun is constantly passing in front of them.

She lets go of me and hugs Nick as if she hasn't seen him in years.

"Mom, this is Lakshmi." Nick presses a proprietary hand to the small of my back, moves me close to him.

"Nick didn't tell us just how beautiful you really are," she says. "We can't wait to see how you put on a sari!"

"Thanks. I own a sari shop." I blush. "Co-own, actually. With my mother." My mother's moment with Mr. Basu floods back to me.

"How amazing! You must be very busy." Mrs. Dunbar is slicing tomatoes and throwing them into a giant salad bowl. "Owning a business is a twenty-four-hour job. Nick knows."

"It is a lot of work—"

"Hell yeah," Jerry pipes in. He starts peeling a cucumber. A man, in the kitchen, cooking with his mother! "Nick's thinking of getting out of the business, aren't you?"

"That's what we should talk about," Nick says.

Nick's thinking of selling his business? My heart flips. What if he no longer drives Asha to the shop? I didn't think the possibility would fill me with such panic.

"Would you like some wine, Lakshmi? We have Merlot," Nick's mother says.

"Wine would be great, thank you!"

She hands me a glass, and the slight bite of the wine spreads through my insides.

A young, red-haired woman comes running in and flings her arms around Nick's neck. She's wearing slippers, sweats, and a sweatshirt. "You made it, Nicky!"

Nicky?

"This is my sister, Fiona," Nick says. "Fiona, Lakshmi."

"You're the famous Lakshmi!" She throws her arms around my neck too, as if we are long-lost cousins, and I take a step backward. Freckles cover her face, some piling together to form one big freckle, and her eyes are the same startling blue as Nick's eyes.

"I'm not famous," I say.

"You are to us." Fiona takes my hand. "I was hoping you'd come. Mom's making lasagna."

"It'll be ready soon," Mrs. Dunbar says. "Get your father in here, will you?"

"He's outside with my husband, Bill," Fiona says. "Showing him the garden, mostly the fruit trees. Dad's always planting new trees. Mom's the flower woman."

"Nick says you're a teacher," I say, trying to make polite conversation.

"Yeah, second grade over at Juan de Fuca. Same school Nick went to. He was a wild kid. He's still wild!"

Nick's off in the corner talking to Jerry.

"Come outside and meet my dad." Still in her clog slippers, she leads me out the back door and across the patio. The backyard is filled with plants and raised gardens, and in the distance, the waning sunlight glints off the ocean. Two tall silhouettes stand near the fruit trees.

"Dad, Bill, come and meet Lakshmi!"

The two men traipse over. Nick's father is taller than Nick, more broad-shouldered, with deep lines in his face and a shock of white hair. He takes my hand in a warm, firm grip. "Pleased to meet you, Lakshmi. You're gonna get cold out here."

Bill is so dark that he could be the coming night. His hand grasping mine makes my skin look pale. "Good to meet you," he says with a slight foreign accent.

"This is Bill, my husband," Fiona says. "I met him while I was in the Peace Corps. He's from Nigeria originally, but he's been here a long time."

I nod, feeling even more comfortable here. It's a relief not to be around relatives who would all be smiling while secretly judging: They would never allow me to date a man such as Bill. They would not approve of Nick, either. Here, I feel strangely liberated.

And Sean, the man who took me to dinner in out-of-the-way restaurants, where his close friends and family wouldn't see that he was dating an Indian.

Here, I don't have to worry.

Even supper is informal. The men yell across the table as

if they're at a football game. They reach over to grab a bowl of green beans, the lasagna, the salt and pepper.

"Nick's the greatest guy you could know," Fiona says, sitting next to me. "He was the kid who helped old ladies cross the street."

"I believe it."

"No, seriously! And the best football player at Juan de Fuca. We all thought he'd make it to the—"

"Fiona," Nick says quickly, then pats his left thigh. He turns to me. "Injured this knee in my senior year. Healed okay, but kept me from playing professionally."

"Oh," I say.

"He was a bit of a speedster too," Fiona whispers. "And a hit with the ladies, what with that convertible—"

"What are you saying?" Nick tries to divide his attention between his brother and us.

"Nothing, don't you worry." Fiona waves a dismissive hand at him, then whispers to me. "He's settled down a lot since high school. Mainly saw this one girl, Liz. But she's kind of stuck-up, so don't worry about her."

"I'm not actually seeing Nick," I say. "He's just a friend."

"Right." Fiona's eyes indicate that she doesn't believe me. "They almost married, but he got cold feet."

I swallow, suddenly going numb. Sita's words haunt me. *Love is marriage.* A man who won't marry can't fall in love.

"So Nick was in love?" I ask. What do I care? I glance at Nick, who's deep in conversation with Jerry.

"I don't know if he ever really loved her. Couldn't give her a ring, but he still sees her once in a while."

Still sees her? "Oh," I say politely and focus on my food. *Couldn't give her a ring.* Nick's love life is none of my business. I'm having a fun evening here while Mr. Basu has kidnapped my mother.

Everyone laughs through supper while Nick's father cracks jokes, and after we finish eating, Nick makes a fire in the living room fireplace. He looks so competent, kneeling in front of the hearth, arranging the logs and kindling, setting them aflame. A warm glow emanates through the room.

I break out the saris, and Fiona and Mrs. Dunbar lead me upstairs to a frilly guest bedroom with lace curtains, where I show Fiona how to wrap an indigo cotton sari.

"Oh, Fiona, you're an exotic princess!" Mrs. Dunbar claps.

"It's all puffy in the front." Fiona frowns in front of the mirror.

"Cotton is like that," I say. "Flatten the pleats like this." I fix the sari, drape the pallu over her shoulder, and tuck it in at her waist.

"Now I love it!" she exclaims, "but how do women wrap these things every day? Saris are so complicated!"

"You get used to it," I say.

"C'mon, Ma, your turn!" Fiona and I dress Mrs. Dunbar in a translucent peach chiffon sari, which promptly slips off and falls in a heap around her ankles. She poses in the petticoat and choli, pretending to be an underwear model. We all burst into laughter.

Finally, I get the sari to stay on.

"You look like a queen, Ma," Fiona says. "But something is missing. Wait! I have just the ticket." She presses a red lipstick bindi into the center of her mother's forehead. "Now you're perfect!"

We traipse downstairs to show off. I carry a couple of extra saris in my arms. The men whistle, and everyone claps.

"Now you, Nick!" Jerry shouts. "Let's see what you look like in a sari."

"No way, not me!" Nick holds up his hands, but Fiona and I are already wrapping a sari around him, tucking it into his jeans and throwing the pallu over his shoulder. He looks comical, a tall, muscular man draped in delicate chiffon. Next, we subject Jerry to the same humiliation, and we're all laughing so hard, we can't breathe.

Later, we all play games—Taboo, Pictionary, Cranium—and laugh again until our bellies hurt. Finally, the family drifts into the dining room for dessert.

"I can't eat another bite," I tell Nick while we're sitting

by the fire. "I'm full of your mother's wonderful lasagna."

"Food is always a huge event for us," Nick says. "Meals go all night—"

"In India too!" I say. "Family events revolve around food. It's the same everywhere."

Nick gives me a funny look. "Yeah."

"Thanks for bringing me here. But I should go soon."

"Don't go." He stokes the flames, rearranging the logs.

"We're leaving for India in a few days. I still have to catch up on work."

"Why do you have to go?"

"Because it's in the stars. Because my father wanted me to meet Ravi. Because I like Ravi. I have to go. I have to know if we get along."

"You and I get along."

"Nick, I like you. We could be friends. You have a wonderful family, but I don't know you very well and—"

"You don't know the Ravi guy at all."

"But our families have known each other for a long time. In India, families are intertwined like branches of a banyan tree."

"What about love? Do you believe in love at first sight?"

My throat goes dry. "Maybe only in the movies. Not in real life."

"Why not in real life?"

"Is that how you felt about Liz?"

"My sister's been talking to you."

"She told me a little."

"I'm talking about you. It's how I feel about you." He looks at me directly, piercing me with those stone-blue eyes.

I'm frozen, my vocal cords disappear. I think back to the moment he walked into the shop, the way the *knowing* dissolved.

Love? What does love feel like? Is it the bowling ball of longing from Mrs. Dasgupta? Ma's golden bubbles when she's around Mr. Basu? Is it this feeling of disorientation? Is it the bubbles that burst from me when Nick's around?

I look away. "You can't possibly love me already."

"Why not? Love is simple, Lakshmi."

"No, it's not."

"I knew the moment I saw you." He grabs my chin and forces me to look at him. Then he gently kisses me, and the sari slips from my shoulder. I'm swept away. Everyone else disappears, and I am lost inside him, wrapped in need, in a world where anything is possible.

"Lakshmi," he whispers against my lips. "You're perfect."

Only the goddess is perfect, divine, entwined with her lover in paradise. Her voice drifts back to me—*Love will be a long and difficult journey.*

I draw back. "Nick, I have to go."

"Wait—give me a chance, Lakshmi."

"Nick, my family, my mother—it's complicated. Love takes time. It has to blossom, to grow."

"So give us some time."

I put on my sweater, and we go outside onto the porch in the cold. "Your sister told me about Liz, and I have to go to India. That was always the plan."

Nick moves closer, until his breath warms my head. "What do you want, Lakshmi? I'm not talking about your family, your mother, what you're supposed to do."

"I want to keep helping people at the store, and I want the business to expand. I love the feel of saris, the fabrics, discovering new designs. I love watching the trends change over time. I love seeing the relieved or ecstatic faces of women when I give them exactly the right sari. And I want to be happy and settle down and have a family one day."

"Don't you think I want the same thing?"

"I don't know what you want, Nick."

"What, I'm not good enough for you?"

"That has nothing to do with it."

"Oh, yes it does. I'm a driver. You're too high class for me, is that it? You have to marry someone from your caste. Am I like one of those untouchables?"

"Nick, no!"

"Think about it. Why won't you give me the time of day?"

"I do, Nick—"

"You hire me to drive, but would you go out with me? Just the two of us?"

"I can't change our plans, Nick. Ma has been looking for the right husband for me for a long time. Arranged marriages do work. I have to give this a try."

"Why? Don't go. Stay with me."

I take off down the steps, my heart racing. Part of me wants to stay with Nick, to throw propriety and promises to the wind, but I can't. The pull of my mother, my father's words in that old, parched letter, and the call of India are far too strong.

Eighteen

When I get home, the house feels different—older and creakier, wiser and darker. Nick drove me in silence, a mountain of ice between us. A lump grows in my throat as I watch him drive away. The *knowing* slips back into me and curls up in the corner of my mind.

This house is no longer the innocent abode of my mother and me. We both have secrets. The images of Ma and Mr. Basu hide in the corners. And I see the shadow of Nick. His kiss lingers on my lips, a ghost.

On the couch, the cats dream their secret dreams. I won't sleep so easily. I'll toss and throw the covers into a Kama Sutra tangle. But I fall into a dreamless slumber.

Sunday evening, Ma is home, reading the newspaper

and sipping tea at the dining table. The setting sun reveals streaks of gold in her graying hair. She's in her usual kurta and slippers, yet she looks not like my mother but like a woman with an invisible life.

"How was your weekend?" she asks. Out-of-focus baubles of happiness play in her mind.

"Fine. The usual." I avoid her gaze. I didn't tell her about my visit with Nick and his family. She doesn't know that I can be as wild as she is. As deceptive.

"You watched some movies last night, nah?" She opens the afternoon newspaper.

"Yes, a movie, Ma. It was about a woman who pretended to be a virgin but who was actually sleeping with some guy she worked with."

"Why on earth would she pretend? Was she married?" Ma peruses the Life & Arts section.

"She had been married once and had been deeply in love, in fact. She even had a child, who still missed the father, and, well, when the child found out—"

"Sounds like the woman had quite a lot of fun." Ma's lips curl into a little secret smile. Why haven't I noticed that smile before? Or perhaps I have, but I didn't understand its true meaning.

"Actually, the man was taking advantage of her. She was lonely and unsure of herself."

"Sounds like a strange movie." She gives me a sharp look.

"How was your weekend, Ma? How was Sonia's?"

Ma pretends to read, but I notice that a clothing ad takes up the whole page. "Lovely—the same as usual."

"How's her arthritis? Her hands?"

"Oh, paining her, paining her as usual." Ma looks up at me, and the bright baubles come into focus. "Everyone is so thrilled for you. They're all saying how happy they are that Ravi Ganguli has shown such interest, which is of course not at all surprising."

"Not at all." I scrape my chair back and go to my room.

Nineteen

*M*onday morning, the shop looks different—brighter, awash with ancestral secrets hidden in the folds of a million saris. The erotic rush of Nick still simmers in my subconscious. *Do you believe in love at first sight?*

I remember Nick's face as he dropped me off and waited for me to go inside my house. I peered past the curtain and saw him standing there. He stayed there a minute before getting into his car and leaving.

I worked up my nerve to confront Mr. Basu, but he's out with the flu. After his wild night seducing my mother!

No matter. Today I visit Chelsea's sister, Lillian. She lives in a modest, blue Cape Cod–style split-level in northeast Seattle. The house is newly painted, and a few large Japanese maples stand in the manicured front yard.

She invites me into her living room, furnished sparsely in soft, pastel colors. Her hair is coiffed, her white blouse and tan slacks perfectly laundered and pressed. An errant, straight hair falls over her forehead. She gives me a brave, weary smile and directs me to a couch. And there, on the carpet, sitting cross-legged and playing with Legos, is the boy I saw in her mind. In person, he's smaller, maybe only four years old. His hair looks finer, like strands of golden silk from a sari.

"This is Jeremy," she says.

"He's beautiful. Hi, Jeremy!"

He doesn't reply, doesn't look up even when the briefcase slips from my hand and lands with a thud. I quickly pick it up.

"How do you like your new house?" I ask him.

"He won't talk to you," Lillian says.

He rocks gently back and forth, intent on the intricate fortress he's building from black and blue Lego pieces.

"That's a cool house, Jeremy," I say.

No answer.

"He's not very social," Lillian says.

"Oh. That's okay. I'm not a huge talker either." Disturbed, I sit on the couch and cross my legs, hoist the briefcase onto the coffee table. A wall of red bricks rises from Jeremy's mind. He's spent his life building that wall, brick by brick, against the unbearable chaos of life outside. He'll do anything to keep that frightening world at bay.

"I see you're still moving in." I point at the stack of boxes sitting unopened in the corner.

"I'm so busy with Jeremy," she says. "He's still getting used to the layout of the rooms, the noise. Too much traffic here. He doesn't like the sound of motorcycles. My husband got the house after our divorce. I couldn't afford to keep it."

"I'm sorry." A cacophony of disjointed images rushes at me—her wedding to a muscular jock, his bewilderment when their son didn't start talking. The slow decay of the marriage. She's put up two pictures of her son on a shelf near the TV.

She sits across from me in an armchair and rubs the palms of her hands together. Her fingernails are bitten to the quick.

I put the briefcase on the table, glance at the large, blank windows overlooking a fenced yard with a swing set.

"You'll want to let the light in," I say. "And go with a soft color. I brought some samples you can hold up to the window, if you like."

"Thank you so much for coming," she says. "Can I get you some tea? I've got some Earl Grey steeping."

"Very kind of you. I'll have a cup."

While she's in the kitchen, I kneel next to Jeremy and watch him building his dream structure. His mind is still a wall, the world outside like a dense mass of unlabeled wires.

"Jeremy, you're going to be all right here," I tell him. He has shut me out, but I catch a glimpse through a crack in the bricks. Inside him lies a heavenly room in smooth blue. Breaths of cartoon cloud blow across that sky.

Lillian returns with tea. "He could read at two, you know. He did arithmetic at three. But no conversations. He didn't say his own name."

"An unusually bright child."

"That's what I thought. To me, he is brilliant. But not to the doctors. He doesn't respond appropriately in social situations, so . . . you'll have to excuse him if he does anything unusual."

"What's appropriate?" I say. "It's all relative."

"We have him in two special programs. I should say, I have him in the programs." Her fingers tremble, and her cup clatters noisily onto the saucer.

Still Jeremy doesn't look up.

"You're very busy and tired," I say. "I hope you're not doing all this alone, taking care of him."

"Oh, no. I have a support group, my mother, my sister, friends. But still—"

"Jeremy's father?"

"He didn't want to have much to do with us when he realized he couldn't play catch or roughhouse without making Jeremy scream—"

Invisible Lives

"Lillian—I have a good feeling. You're strong, and—"

That's when the motorcycle roars by, the engine noise reverberating through the house. Jeremy covers his ears and lets out a pure animal screech. The sound terrifies me, and it goes on and on, not stopping as he rocks back and forth, screaming and screaming.

I put my tea on the coffee table. I should leave—I don't belong in this family moment. But I can't go.

Lillian takes Jeremy's hand and whisks him down the hall, into another room, slamming the door. I'm in the empty living room alone, the Legos strewn across the carpet. I pace, my fingers curled into fists. Why am I here? Why did I feel compelled to bring the shop to Lillian's house if I can't help?

The screaming waxes and wanes, and I hear Lillian's voice in between, soothing in a practiced, weary way. *Damn her husband, damn fate,* I'm thinking. A beautiful boy, so sensitive, thrown into life without a buffer to help him make sense of the world.

I grab my samples and stuff them back into the briefcase, and then I see it. The sky-blue cotton sari with puffs of candy-cotton cloud. How did that get into the briefcase? I tiptoe down the hall and knock on the bedroom door.

The screaming has died down to a rhythmic moaning. "Come in," Lillian says. "I'm so sorry about this. Usually our neighbor with the motorcycle has left for work by now."

159

"I'm sorry for intruding." I step into the semidarkness.

Jeremy's room isn't what he wants. It's pale green with a yellow border. His comforter is green too.

"Blue," I say. "He needs a blue room. Blue like the sky."

She gives me a curious look. "How did you know about the sky-room?"

"I—"

"The only words he says often are 'sky room.' When he looks up at the sky. How did you know that?"

"I didn't. He looks like a boy who enjoys a clear day."

He's still moaning, rocking back and forth on the bed.

"Jeremy, I have a present for you," I say. "I know it was your birthday recently. You got some presents from your aunt Chelsea and other people, and I have one for you today."

Lillian gives me a questioning look.

I place the sari gently on the bed in front of Jeremy. The moaning instantly stops, and he stares at the sari as if watching a fantastic, private circus. He's quiet and still, floating away in his sky-room.

Twenty

Tuesday morning, Mr. Basu is still out sick. I wonder if he caught a chill in Vancouver. While I'm unfurling new saris, a disheveled woman bursts into the shop, her thoughts like tiny wild animals darting into shadows. She's wearing jeans and a Seattle T-shirt underneath a windbreaker, and she's carrying a suitcase, her long, black hair a windswept mess.

"Ms. Lakshmi?" She runs over to me, the suitcase banging against her leg. Her voice drops to a whisper. "You told me I could talk to you whenever I need help. I need to talk to you right away."

"Sita! I hardly recognized you! Are you all right? Where's your mother?"

A runaway look lives in her eyes. "Ma's at home. I've left."

"You've left?" I drop my voice to a whisper.

"Everything I own. Everything I need is here." She glances at the suitcase.

"Come, we can walk to Cedarlake Café." I give Ma the signal that I'm taking a break and hurry Sita to the café. The smells of scones and freshly brewed coffee fill the air, and a thin strain of Bob Dylan croons in the background. Marcus winks at me, but I'm in no mood to flirt. We order drinks—Sita tea and me a double latte—and sit at a couch away from the window.

"What's going on, Sita?" I ask. "Did you fight with your parents?"

Marcus glances over with curiosity.

Sita grips the teacup as if it might fly away. Her thoughts scream out in a jumble of nerves. "My bedroom at home, you know, has a silk bedspread and photos of all my cousins on the dresser."

"Sita—"

"The wedding is . . . was to be in Mumbai." Her fingers tremble so much that the liquid sloshes from the cup. "Please don't tell anyone. Don't tell my parents. I'm twenty-three. I'm not a minor."

"Tell them what? Are you in . . . trouble?"

She bites her lip. Why can't I see into her mind? Has Nick's influence spilled over into my everyday life?

Her glance flits around the room. She's in flux, her

thoughts shifting in currents. "I've decided not to marry Kishor. My parents won't listen."

"You're nervous about the wedding."

"When I think of living with him in India, I feel sick." She stares out the window at a vision out of reach.

"Sita." I try to take her hand, but it's securely fastened to the teacup. "Don't you want a huge wedding? Your parents will worry about you. Families have fights, but they always reconcile. Maybe you just need a little time."

"I've had all the time in the world." Her thoughts gather and she sits straighter, taking a deep breath. "Don't you see? I never wanted to marry him. I've done what I was supposed to do all my life. I can't go back." Tears spill from her eyes. "But where do I go?"

"Sita—it's okay." I put my arms around her, feel her body trembling. "What about going back to your parents for now?"

I've done what I was supposed to do all my life.

She draws away. "You don't understand. They want this match more than anything. I need a place to go for a while."

I sit back, overwhelmed. She's just turned on to a highway with no signs, and I can't show her the way. "Look, why don't we try to talk to your parents—"

"I can't go back, not now."

"Okay, look. We'll figure out something. I'll be right back. Stay here."

I run next door, take Ma into the back room, and explain the situation. For now, her episode with Mr. Basu recedes. Surely with her own clandestine activities, she'll understand Sita.

Ma's lips purse into a tight line, and her face goes hard. "Does she think she can just run off?"

"She wants to pursue her own dreams." There, where did that come from?

"Her poor mother must be in shock," Ma says. "And her father—I can't even begin to imagine."

"Ma, she needs a place to go."

"I won't have that girl under my roof."

"Just until things settle down—"

"These things don't settle down, Bibu. They only become worse." A shadow falls over Ma's happy thoughts.

"She's distraught, Ma. What about her feelings, about what she wants?"

"I'm sure the family took all that into account, but by leaving this way she has disgraced her parents and left them in quite a fix. They've invited hundreds of guests to the wedding."

"What does the wedding matter if she doesn't love the man?" I yell, then cover my mouth. "I didn't mean to shout."

"I will not tolerate a runaway bride in my home. Do what you like, Bibu. There will be no Sita in our house."

"All right, Ma, I'll figure out something else."

"The best you can do for her is take her home." She lifts her sari and rushes back into the store.

Fifteen minutes later, Mitra, Sita, and I are in Mitra's car heading into town, Sita in the backseat. She leans against the headrest, and a great blanket of fatigue emanates from her mind.

"You can sleep in my room, honey!" Mitra shouts. "I'll take the couch!" The car careens over two lanes of traffic, and Sita jolts upright, suddenly alert.

"Mitra, you'll get us all killed," I say, but my heart isn't in it.

We make it to her apartment intact. She still lives as if in a college dorm, the arrangement of furniture haphazard. Mitra leaves bras thrown over chairs, woven wool blankets draped over the back of the couch.

"I sleep in on weekends," Mitra announces, taking Sita's suitcase to the bedroom. "And I snore through anything. So don't worry about waking me up."

"You are too kind, Ms. Mehta," Sita says.

"Oh, call me Mitra!" She comes close to me and whispers, "My father is coming to my dance performance!"

I smile and squeeze her arm.

"Shouldn't we call your parents, Sita?" I say. "Just to put their minds at ease?"

"I don't want to talk to them." But she writes the number

on a slip of paper and hands it to me, her fingers trembling.

My heart pounds as I punch in the numbers.

"Hallo?" a hollow male voice answers.

"Mr. Dutta? This is Lakshmi Sen, from the sari shop?"

"Yes?"

"I want you to know that your daughter, Sita, came to me, and she's staying with my friend Mitra for a while—"

"She is all right? I've been so worried! Where is she?"

"She's fine, a bit confused." I glance at Sita and mouth the words, *"Your father."* She nods and lets out a breath.

Then I hear a scrambling, and her mother screeches on the line. "This is Mrs. Dutta. Who is this and what do you want?"

I repeat what I told Sita's father.

"I don't know of whom you speak," Mrs. Dutta says in a cold voice.

"Sita, your daughter."

"What daughter? I once had a daughter, but—"

"Mrs. Dutta, she's really upset."

"I don't have a daughter. Don't call here again." Mrs. Dutta hangs up.

Twenty-one

$\mathcal{I}$'m reeling when I return to the shop. I left Sita crying, while Mitra tried to comfort her with soothing words and tea. I have to pretend that all's well. I have to hope that Mrs. Dutta is just having a bad day and that she'll come around, but I have doubts.

I don't have a daughter.

I'm hoping to hide in the office for a while, but as soon as I open the door, I know that Nick is here. Huge sparkling bubbles hover in the air. I swat them away, but oh, how he looks in a pressed black suit, and I'm instantly jealous of Asha, who gets to be with him all day.

She's brought a group of friends, and Ma and Pooja are beside themselves. They don't even notice Nick pull me aside and whisper in my ear. "Lakshmi, I've missed you," he says.

"Nick, not here." I look straight ahead, pretend to arrange some scarves.

"Why not here?"

I don't have a daughter.

"All right," he says. "I just want you to know. I want to keep seeing you."

My face heats, and Ma glances my way. I deliberately drop a scarf and bend to pick it up, my face hidden by the rows of clothing. When I stand, I turn to face the shelves of saris along the wall. "Nick, don't talk about this now."

There's a half smile on Nick's face, but he goes instantly blank when Ma rushes over to us. "Lakshmi! Today is the day we pick Asha's wedding sari!"

My fingers curl into fists. The saris offer no hints, no images. Only the blinding bubbles. The *knowing* is stone-walling me. Memories of Nick fill the space all around me. And Sita's tears, and her mother's cold voice.

I have to focus. Saris. "Nick," I whisper. "You have to get out of here."

"Why? So you can pretend you never met me?" He glances over at Asha, who's sifting through the silk scarves.

"Because I need to choose a sari for Asha."

"You can't do that with me here?"

"You don't need to be here. Go and wait in the car. I

can't . . . think when you're here. And why do you need to be in here, anyway?"

"Lakshmi, is everything all right?" Ma calls from the other side of the room. I'm grateful that the acoustics muffle my words, that a conversation here can't be heard from where she's standing.

"Fine, Ma! We're discussing Asha's wedding." I turn my back on Nick.

How can I explain the *knowing*, that it slips down the drain when he's around? Then I hear the door swing open and shut as he leaves. For a moment, a lonely wind sweeps through my heart, but I push it away as the *knowing* waltzes back in again.

Saris.

What would Asha consider most beautiful? She likes to stand out. I pick a red silk wedding sari with the most inlaid gold. But not *too* pretentious. Asha isn't showy. She prefers style, elegance. Maybe the violet sari with an intricately woven border. Or the shimmering vermilion with a medium amount of gold and a yellow undertone, like sunshine. Yes. Perfect!

But is it?

I glance toward the closed door. No sign of Nick. I can't see him loitering on the sidewalk, hands in his pockets. I can't see the limousine. I should be thrilled. The *knowing* dances in circles, crystal clear. Snippets of longings sprinkle into my mind, and yet they don't coalesce into a coherent picture. The bubbles, my annoying emotions are still in the way. Worry and longing tumble around in my heart. I want to run outside and apologize to Nick. How can I explain to him the pull of family, of my father? I feel Baba's eternal breath on my shoulder, gently steering me toward Ravi Ganguli. How can I make Nick understand the importance of history, of tradition?

What will I do? The *knowing* clings to me, but my thoughts are outside in the rain, with Nick.

Focus.

I pull all three saris off the shelf, then more saris and more—

"All of these?" Asha says. "But which would be best for me, Lakshmi?"

"Lakshmi? Are you feeling quite all right?" Ma asks, stepping close to me.

I'm thinking of Nick's breath in my ear. *Do you believe in love at first sight?*

"What is all this you are giving me?" Asha says in a low voice.

"I have to pull out several before I can, um, narrow it down," I say. The *knowing* should've saved me when Nick walked out. But I'm lost.

"I see. Then do your thing and I'll stay out of your way."

"No, don't do that," I say. "I mean, don't stay out of the

way. The sari is for you. What's your favorite color, and do you want to go with traditional or daring?"

I've never asked questions before. Ma goes pale.

"I'm open to all colors," Asha says. "You choose."

"But this is your wedding—"

"And you are the expert. My favorite color is yellow, but of course I can't wear yellow at my wedding. Do I want everyone to think I am pregnant?" She laughs.

"That's what I thought, of course." No help, no help at all! I stare at the heap.

"Lakshmi? What do you see?" Ma says, a thread of pure anxiety in her voice.

"I see—a traditional wedding with a modern edge."

"Edge, yes." Asha nods.

I close my eyes and try to concentrate, but the images hide just out of reach. I open my eyes to the bright lights, to everyone staring at me. I pick up the vermilion silk, the one with medium inlay and a yellow undertone.

No, I'm not sure. I drop it.

My hand moves to the violet. . . .

"Purple? Are you sure?" Asha's lips turn down. "I hate purple. Reminds me of grapes."

"I meant to give you another one." Tears press at the backs of my eyes. The store falls into a hush. A vast sea of saris undulates before my eyes, floating off into oblivion.

"Lakshmi, which one did you mean to give me?"

I can't move. Which one?

I pick up a pink sari and hand it to Asha.

"You're thinking pink?" She taps her finger on her chin.

"Innocent and yet bold," I lie. The bubbles of longing for Nick are in the way, but how can I tell her?

"Fine, we'll try it," Asha says. "Now Pooja, bring me that sleeveless choli, will you?"

But when Asha emerges from the dressing room, the sari resembles a puffy dollop of cotton candy. Everyone falls silent.

Asha's face tightens, and Ma presses a hand to her chest.

"This is your idea of the perfect wedding sari," Asha says. "Bordello pink." Her eyes sear holes through my forehead.

"I thought—"

"Don't speak." She glares at herself in the mirror. Never has a sari looked so awful. The undertone of gray gives her face a deathly pallor. "I look hideous," she says. "I heard so much about you, Lakshmi. But my sister is right. You are a fraud."

"Please, I'm sure it was just a test sari," Ma says, rushing forward.

Tears sting my eyes.

"Pink is a new style, not at all traditional," Pooja says. "We are trying it out on you. Like the guinea pig for the new saris!"

"Pooja!" Ma shouts.

I'm frozen, the *knowing* laughing at me from somewhere beyond reach. My confusion about Nick must've tackled the *knowing* and jumbled it up.

"You're calling me a guinea pig?" Asha says.

Oh, disaster. I rush forward, finding my feet again. "She didn't mean that. I can show you other ones—"

"No!" Asha raises her hand. "I can no longer trust your judgment."

"She's been ill," Ma says. "Why not try the other ones?"

"I don't have time for this," Asha says.

"We've ordered many fabrics, and the seamstress is beginning work," Ma says. "We can give you a discount!"

"I'll compensate you for what you've already done," Asha says coldly. "Money is no problem."

"Your wedding sari can be easily found," Ma says, taking my arm.

"I'll look elsewhere," Asha says.

Ma pales. "But—"

"I'm sorry, Mrs. Sen, but please cancel my orders. I'm taking my business elsewhere."

Twenty-two

"I'm so sorry, Ma," I say over supper. I made an elaborate meal, and she's eating one grain of rice at a time. I expected her to yell at me, but she's quiet.

"It's all right, Bibu," she says in a tired voice. "Perhaps I've put too much pressure on you. And besides, it was bound to happen. Asha Rao is so demanding, she would've fired us at some point anyway."

I think of what Nick said on the way back from the set. Asha fires all her assistants. "But still, Ma, my mind was in a jumble. I could've tried to concentrate."

Ma puts her hand over mine. "Bibu, you think the world rests on your shoulders, but it doesn't. You don't have to know everything all the time."

I sit back, relief and sadness pressing on me. Have I felt the weight of the world on my shoulders? Of Mitra, Nisha, Sita? Our customers? I think of Lillian and her son, Jeremy. I wonder what they're doing, whether Jeremy is playing with Legos at this moment. "I don't know everything and I can't help everyone," I whisper.

"Try having a little fun," Ma says. "We'll have fun in India, nah? You'll love Ravi. We'll have lovely food, go shopping, visit the relatives."

"Of course, Ma."

A strange image emerges from her mind. She's standing on a mountaintop, the wind playing with her hair, Mr. Basu behind her.

I take her hand. "I'll make it up to you."

"We must put the shop up for sale."

"What?" I let go of her hand.

She looks at me with tears in her eyes, but her thoughts are opaque. "I've been thinking about it a long time, Lakshmi. You'll marry. Ravi is a doctor. You don't need the shop. You're trapped there—you always feel a need to help people, but I want you to be happy. You, Bibu."

"Oh, Ma, but we've always had the shop!" The bottom drops out of my heart.

She lets out a long sigh. "It is time."

"You love the shop, Ma. You love saris."

"Perhaps I must retire. I don't know."

"Don't talk that way. Don't even think that way. We'll get more good accounts, good business. You'll see. Don't give up."

She pats my hand and takes a long sip of water. "We'll worry about this later, nah?"

That night, I dream of ripped saris, of Ma and me standing in an empty shop, cobwebs in our hair, and then the cobwebs dissolve into dust, and I'm on the teeming Mumbai streets. I dream of chapatis cooked over open flames, of sparkling Limca soft drinks and noisy cinemas. I dream of gauzy mosquito nets and soft white sand beaches and palm trees and spicy cologne. I dream of my grandmother, my cousins, my aunts and uncles, and the ghosts of ancestors I never knew. I dream of India.

Twenty-three

*C*all me the Jet-setting World Traveler with the Sixth Sense. In India, I let down my hair and lose the glasses. The *knowing* exhausts itself into a stupor, overstimulated by the sheer mass of humanity. I've been watching an endless collage of colorful images, like shards of light in a kaleidoscope. This is worse than New York.

One woman brushes my arm in the street, and I see her pick up a little boy in a garden full of roses. I know he's dead. There's too much light, the garden perfect. A man touches my arm, and I see him riding a bike along a white sand beach—perhaps in Goa, perhaps in Chennai, a young woman on the bicycle beside him. Pink petals fall from the sky.

Here, Ma and I temporarily forget that we've put the shop up for sale, forget that we've left Mr. Basu and Pooja in charge. I didn't have time to talk to him, but Ma's weekend with him feels small now, a blip in the scheme of time.

We may return to disaster in America, but for now, I have to meet Ravi Ganguli. Ma doesn't know—I've brought the gold ring, the one Nick found. I keep it on a chain around my neck, hidden beneath my shirt. I keep it for luck and to remember him, although he is now my past.

We stay in Ma's elder sister's flat in Alipore. It's replete with swirling scents of sandalwood and ancient spices. Auntie Bee must've been cooking for two days in anticipation of our arrival. Her husband, Uncle Goola, spends his days working at his engineering firm until late into the evening. The ghosts of my relatives whisper in the shadows, and the gods seem to fit here, living in their statues and paintings.

Auntie herself, adorned in a blue chiffon sari, has aged. She's like a pebble on the beach. The wind and tides have scoured her to a smooth finish, only the threads and lines of her past run through her skin, telling stories. Her daughter, Prithi, barely into her teens, spends all her time reading.

Here, relatives gather for elaborate meals. I reunite with cousins and aunts and uncles, and we talk of our lives far into the night, and I begin to forget I ever had a life in America. I think only of Ravi Ganguli coming to meet Ma and me tomorrow. Everyone else will leave to allow us a few moments alone.

When Ravi appears at the door, he's beyond handsome. In person, he appears poised and suave, his face lean, the bones defined, and yet there's a glint of playfulness on his full lips. He brings the hint of the Hindu gods, the breath of ancestors, the spice and swirl of ancient India. He's slim and so regal that the furniture recedes into drab obscurity, and I have the urge to curtsy before him. If it weren't for my hand gripping the doorknob, I would fall to my knees. Instead I'm trapped in his gaze, lost in his eyes, which are the deep black of a moonless midnight. And inside that darkness, love stories unfold in unknown shadows.

He's in a kurta and pajama, complete and uncompromised in his Indian-ness, and I'm awestruck, speechless. I nearly forget that I let down my hair and put on lipstick, that black kajal rims my eyes and I'm wearing a pale blue churidar kurta. His gaze lingers on the shirt's intricate embroidery, travels down the pants to the narrow cuffs. Vague wisps of memory emanate from him—white Indian sunlight dispersing in dust, a mansion on the outskirts of Delhi.

"You must be Lakshmi," he says warmly. "You're even more beautiful than in your picture."

I blush. "And so are you." I can't speak properly. Then I remember my manners. "Oh, you're standing in the doorway. How rude of me, please come in." I step aside to let him into the foyer, then close the door after him. The ghosts of his entourage clamor outside—the hints of servants, drivers, his royal subjects. He's a man who should be surrounded by helpers.

"I've been waiting for this moment," he says, taking my hands in his. His fingers are dry and warm. Anticipation breathes from his skin, wanders up my arms. Then he lets go of my hands, and the sensation disappears. "I thought of this meeting for days." His gaze doesn't waver from my eyes. "I am not disappointed."

"Neither am I." I bite my lip, and heat rushes through my cheeks. "Mr. Ganguli. I've been so looking forward—"

"Call me Ravi, please." His mind sweeps me into our own private moment. He's the scent I seek, a tantalizing coattail disappearing around a corner.

"How wonderful to see you. Come in, come in." Ma's rushing out from the kitchen. "Oh my, Mr. Ganguli. You are most welcome here."

"I'm honored," Ravi says. "And you're both looking so beautiful."

"We hope you're comfortable. We'll have *cha*. You haven't already had tea, have you?"

"Cha would be lovely." He smiles.

"Do sit—make yourself at home." Ma lets out a tiny, embarrassed giggle. "I've got Darjeeling, second flush."

"Sounds lovely." Ravi does not sit. "Please do let me help. You must be terribly tired."

"No need. We have servants." Ma's bursting with admiration for this man, her approval popping out in daisies all around her.

"Ma, please, let me help—"

"No, no. You two make yourselves comfortable. This is your time together." Ma pats the air, gesturing for us to sit.

Ravi and I give each other knowing looks—*parents*—and sit while Ma bustles off to clank around in the kitchen.

Ravi folds into a chair as if he's always lived here. He surveys the room, then rests his gaze on me. I'm on the couch, my hands clasped in my lap.

"You're even lovelier in person," Ravi says. Nothing but blue sincerity emanates from him—blue with an exotic, woven border and just beyond, an exciting, unknowable future.

"You're better in person too," I say. "Not that you looked like chopped liver in your pictures, mind you. But my computer monitor doesn't have the highest resolution."

He chuckles, easing over my discomfort, and we exchange pleasantries, asking after each other's families and health and jobs, our words dancing in the air, doing a waltz around each other while our eyes lock.

"Tell me—how long have you and your ma lived in America?" he asks.

"Since just after I was born—my father died many years ago, as you know."

"It must have been very difficult for you to lose him."

"I was young. I don't remember much about him."

"It doesn't matter what age you were." His voice is gentle. "It is still a great loss. A father is so important to the well-being of a child."

I bite my lip. "He started teaching me to ride a bike with training wheels—"

"As all fathers do, and as I will do with my children." He gives me a warm smile and I melt.

"Baba embraced American traditions. He brought home a Christmas tree and hung Christmas lights. I remember seeing him on the ladder. Ma and I don't do that anymore. She's too busy, and I'm afraid of standing on high ladders. But Christmas is coming soon—"

"Not to worry." Ravi leans forward and in one swift movement takes my hands in his again. I'm comforted by his touch, by the caring caress of his fingers. "We rarely celebrate Christmas at my home in any case."

I see no artifice inside him, and the *knowing* remains intact. "You're too kind."

Ma bangs and clangs in the kitchen to remind us that she's there but not listening. Oh, no, never listening.

"You still miss your Baba, even after all these years."

"Of course—I still miss him. I have a photo of him in

my room, actually. And I keep the last letter he wrote to me, while he was in the train heading up to see you—"

"Ah yes. I recall hearing of the . . . accident." Ravi stares off as if looking back to that moment.

Accident.

My father died in an accident.

I've always known this, but somehow Ravi's saying it makes it more real. The backs of my eyes sting with the threat of tears. Ravi and his parents waited at the other end of the line for a train that would never come.

His touch holds the secrets of past and future.

A lump comes into my throat. "I was very small—only seven. I kept expecting him to come home."

"He loved to walk in our gardens in Darjeeling." Ravi lets go of my hands and leans back. "I remember him well. He brought me sweets every time he visited. *Sandesh* and—"

"—*Roshogollas*. He brought them to me as well," I exclaim. "He used to hide them in his suitcase and smuggle them through customs. They were squished by the time he got home, but they still tasted like heaven."

"Nothing like squished roshogollas." Ravi laughs, and we're both silent for a moment. "He was a wonderful man," Ravi says. "He and my father would spend hours in the drawing room, drinking whisky and laughing and talking. We all walked on the trails near our house—"

"I wish I could remember him the way you do. I wish he'd brought me with him."

"But then you might not be here today," Ravi says in a soft voice. "And that would be a tragedy."

When we sit down to dinner, he keeps the flirtation going with his eyes. He praises the curry, aloo gobi, and basmati rice. The soft lilt of his accent touches my soul.

"Your husband remembered every detail of everything he ever read," Ravi tells Ma. "He would recite statistics and obscure facts while drinking his morning cha—"

"I can't believe you have such a memory of him!" Ma says, her eyes bright. "Oh, Dr. Ganguli—"

"Call me Ravi." He gives a charming smile.

"It's such a pleasure to know a man like you, so closely tied to our family," Ma says, her voice low and husky, still grief-stricken after all these years, and yet another shadow pops into her mind. A round shadow, with two hairs sticking up on its head. Then she banishes the thought, even from herself.

I nearly choke on my rice.

"You must come to our estates for a visit," Ravi says, giving me a quick wink.

Ma beams and replies in Bengali, clearly thrilled. "How I would love to come. Thank you for the kind invitation."

"We should love to have you." His gaze lingers on me. "I can't imagine a better meal," he says finally, leaning back to dab his face with the cloth napkin. It took me forever to find the good napkins in the kitchen drawers.

"It was actually Lakshmi who made the food," Ma says. "I added the finishing touches, with the cook."

He raises his eyebrows at me. He's impressed. "You're a wonderful cook as well as beautiful." He imagines taking me to meet his family, holding my elbow as we walk into the drawing room.

"When are you coming to America?" Ma asks.

"Just finalizing the details." Ravi gives me a long look. "I've taken a position at Cedar View Hospital in Seattle. And I should like to have a wife. One gets very lonely without companionship."

"I can imagine!" Ma's beaming, looking from Ravi to me. "And Lakshmi gets lonely as well."

"Oh, Ma—"

None of us speaks of all the factors that make Ravi and me a perfect match, or the auspicious date chosen by Ravi's family astrologer. We know all this already—the meeting is to see if Ravi and I like each other.

He rises, kisses the back of my hand on the way out, and I become Princess Anjuli from the *Far Pavilions*.

"I'd like to take you for dinner tomorrow, at the Taj Mahal restaurant," he says. "I'll bring the car at seven."

After he leaves, Ma collapses on the couch, fanning herself. "Oh, Lakshmi! I am beside myself! My palpitations!"

"Ma, you don't have palpitations." I sit beside her and take her hands in mine. Warmth and comfort come from her, and a thick golden excitement.

"If I had palpitations, they'd be flaring now. How could we have asked for better luck? Oh, Lakshmi, this time next year, you'll be happily married!"

Twenty-four

At the Taj, Ravi acts like a prince, escorting me from the car, holding my elbow in the five-star hotel. At a table draped in satin, he runs his thumbs across the palms of my hands. I put on a mauve churidar kurta, but he's dressed casually today, in jeans, a white cotton shirt open at the neck, and a blue sports jacket.

"I want to know everything about you," Ravi says.

"And I you—"

"We have all the time in the world."

"Not if your parents have chosen an auspicious date."

"The date is flexible. Should I ask your favorite color, food, drink?"

"Red, samosas, and mango lassi. And you?"

"Turquoise, biryani, and mango lassi."

I smile and glance at the Indian waiters, their brown skin in sharp contrast to their pressed white uniforms as they balance trays on their fingertips. They don't need the Mango Bay Tanning Salon in Cedarlake. They don't even know Cedarlake exists. My first evening with Nick flashes into my mind—the wind in Port Gamble, his leg against mine in the tearoom.

The waiter brings mango lassis—mango juice and yogurt. Ravi releases my hands and sits back, regarding me. He's cool, collected. He takes a swig of lassi. "You're dedicated to helping your ma. Even when you could be out pursuing your own career, using your degree to get ahead."

"I wouldn't consider any other path. I've always been with Ma." *I've done what I was supposed to do all my life.*

I wonder about Sita. Is she moping in Mitra's apartment? Has Rina's mother-in-law returned to India? Has Mitra contacted her father? I wonder about Jeremy. My token offering, the sari with the sky-room pattern, could only serve as a temporary soother. And I think of Nick, driving Asha all over town, but not to our shop.

"It's nice to be here without the families, isn't it?" Ravi says, and I nod. "A century ago, we would not have even met before the wedding. Our parents would've made the arrangements."

"Should we unmeet each other?" I sip my lassi, the liquid sweet and cool on my tongue. I'm thrown back in time to my great-grandmother peering through a burgundy veil at the blurry face of her husband, a handsome man whom she'd never seen but with whom she would sleep that very night.

"I would never unmeet you," Ravi says. "Even if I had a time machine."

I'm floating on a bed of invisible satin, but the voice that plays in my head is Nick's. The deep rumble, the hint of a drawl—no!

The waiter brings us an appetizer of samosas, triangles of pastry filled with potato curry and peas and cauliflower. Thankful for the distraction, I dip my samosa in a bowl of red sauce and take a tentative bite. The fire-hot spiciness blazes in my mouth. Ravi devours the samosa without flinching.

"We're the right match for each other." His voice grows thick. "Our histories are entwined like the branches of a banyan tree—" He clears his throat. "This is something our families have wanted."

What my father would've wanted. "Yes."

"Why wait?" he asks.

I've been holding my breath again, and now I let out the air.

"Lakshmi, marry me."

How could I ask for a more romantic moment, time

stretched across the twilight sky in five shades of toxic red?

"Marry you?" I parrot, the words mushy through my half-chewed mouthful of samosa. *Do you believe in love at first sight?*

He's patient, his eyes watchful.

"How kind of you to ask," I say shakily, as if he's just offered me his seat on a train. *He just asked you to marry him, you dolt!* But my mouth won't say yes, although everything he says is true. "Let me think about it." Someone else is talking.

He doesn't blink, doesn't miss a beat. "Of course, don't feel pressure. If you do, then perhaps it is not the right time."

And instantly, I'm falling off a cliff into a near-death experience. I hang onto the precipice and pull myself up over the ledge. "Just give me a minute—"

"No need to explain." I sense no animosity in his mind, no uncertainty.

My one chance to marry someone who fits with me exactly, in age, in social status. Our match is auspicious, and yet—why can't I say yes? Is it because of Nick? A man who is wrong for me in every way? A man who dives in without thinking, who thinks he's in love when he doesn't truly know me?

And I don't know Ravi, but such matches have been made for generations. I should not hesitate.

"I'm not feeling well." I stand, suddenly dizzy.

Ravi stands and reaches me in a long stride, grabbing my elbow. "Must be the heat."

"I should . . . go back to my aunt's house."

"Of course, I'll have the car brought around. Come."

Twenty-five

*B*ack at Auntie Bee's flat, I hold my secret close to my chest, although the news of Ravi's proposal will likely reach here at the speed of a nuclear-powered rickshaw. Ma and Auntie are visiting friends, so I have a minute to breathe. I escape to my room and flop on the bed. The glass doors stand open to the balcony, letting thick, smoky air waft in. Soft laughter kicks up from the streets.

Marry me.

The words sit like gems in the satin of my brain, their beauty and brightness luring me. I need to talk to a friend, but I've left everyone behind in Seattle.

I fumble in my purse for my cell phone, flip it open. I don't get service here, but I long to call Mitra or Nisha.

They'll tell me to marry him, no questions asked, won't they?

I try not to imagine Nick's body, his broad shoulders. Then Ravi's smooth voice flows into my mind, his easy manner, his slim but solid build. He comes from a good family, a strong background. He understands the intricacies and nuances of Bengali families. He's a good man, handsome.

Love blossoms over many years, the way my cousin Prithi has blossomed. She bounces into the room. She's still wiry in jeans and a white blouse, the glasses slipping down her nose, a book sprouting from her fingers, a slight mustache growing on her upper lip. Oh, I forgot the Nair.

This is the fate of Indian girls, to have their black hair show up starkly against their skin. Prithi's mother, Auntie Bee, bleaches her upper lip. The bushy hair turned orange and now draws the utmost attention, a little orange flag.

"What are you reading, Prithi?" I ask.

She waves the book. *Pride and Prejudice.* Yesterday it was *Beyond Indigo.* She reads everything from mysteries to romances, thrillers and biographies. She reads the backs of cereal boxes, bottles, the inserts that come with boxed perfumes or soaps. Right now she's reading the look in my eyes as she jumps on the bed next to me.

"He popped the big question," she said.

"How do you know?" I can't help but smile at her sensitivity. Runs in the family.

"You look different, like someone turned you inside out."

"You've always had a way with words." I touch her hair, caught and tamed into a ponytail.

"Omigod!" she squeals and presses her face into a pillow, letting out muffled screams. Then she throws the pillow at me. "You are such a lucky duck! Have you told your ma? Have you told my ma? Nona? Lakshmi's getting married!"

"Whoa, not so fast. Don't tell anyone. I haven't said yes."

"But why not?" She looks up at me in utter amazement. "He's a dreamboat. My friends are all talking about him."

"Just because he's a dreamboat doesn't mean I should marry him."

She sits close, our shoulders touching. In India, personal space means half a centimeter. She gives off the slight smell of soap and unwashed hair. "So have you, you know, kissed him?"

"Kissed him—of course." I'm lying. Am I supposed to wait for our wedding night? What secrets would a kiss reveal? I think of Nick's kisses, the way I floated.

"Have you done anything else, Lakshmi-didi?" Prithi's eyes widen as she addresses me as "didi," elder sister, while asking me an inappropriately intimate question.

"Prithi, are you supposed to know about such things?"

"I learned in school. I'm not stupid."

"We have not done anything more, and we probably won't—what if I don't marry him? Then I'll regret doing anything . . . more with him. You remember that, okay? Have you kissed a boy?"

Her face goes red. "At the dance. But now I like a different boy, but I don't know if he likes me." She flips her ponytail. "I want to cut my hair and get contact lenses, but Ma won't let me."

"Wait until you're older. You don't need to attract boys just yet. You can keep reading, okay?"

She pouts, glancing down at her book, and pushes the glasses up on her nose.

"We're going to a party tomorrow afternoon," Prithi says. "Another American cousin has come. Chandra. She lives in New York now. She's an artist, just now married—"

"Why didn't I know about her?"

"She went to the States for her studies a few years back," Prithi says. "Now she is oh, such an American. She has married an American, an artist."

When Ma and Auntie return in a rush of perfume and gossip, Ma races in and hugs me. "Ah, you are getting married, my sweet!" She's at home here in her chiffon saris, the many rings on her fingers, the sindoor in her hair part. She doesn't walk—she undulates, the folds and creases of her sari like an ocean of ripples and waves.

"Is it true? Has Ravi asked you to marry him?" Auntie

Bee asks and takes my hands. I catch a flashing image of her tangled in bed with Uncle Goola—truly tangled, since her hair is so long. I let go of her hands and dispel the image. I've learned which pictures to toss and which to file.

"What did you tell him?" Ma, Auntie, and cousin Prithi gather around the bed and stare at me as if I'm a new species of house gecko.

"I told him I had to think about it," I say.

"Think, what thinking is needed?" Ma shrieks.

"Make him squirm for a bit. Good girl," Auntie Bee says.

Then my grandmother, Nona, shuffles in wearing a long kaftan, her smoky white hair sticking out in all directions. If you didn't know she was the hottest spice on the rack, you might think of her as a crazy bag lady. But Nona's far from crazy. Ma inherited her clear mind and stamina.

Nona sits on the bed next to me, pats a gnarled brown hand on my knee. "I have heard all this ruckus and commotion," she says in a gravelly voice. "And I am saying that you will know that this is right."

"We all know you've been looking and looking for such a long time," Ma says. "Ravi's a great man."

"Ma—thanks. I really don't know what to do." Tears prick the backs of my eyes.

"You already know!"

"I should marry him, right?" I ask. "It's what—" My

voice trails off. What Baba would've wanted. Even after all these years, I don't want to mention my father. A hole opens in her heart when I talk about him.

"The main thing is for you to be happy," Ma says. "Ravi will make you happy. You'll see!"

"You must go to see your Thakurma," Nona says quietly. "She will have the answer."

Thakurma, my father's mother. The last time I saw her, she resided nearly full-time in her bungalow in the northern foothills, in the company of her cook, her driver, and a plethora of part-time helpers. She spent her days tending her gardens.

Ma gives me a look. "We'll go, Bibu."

After they leave the room, Prithi gets back on the bed and sits very close again, as if she needs to touch my arm to know I'm here. "The main thing is for you to be happy," she parrots in a somber voice. "Ravi might be the love of your life, or he might not. You might one day be walking down the street and you'll meet the love of your life and you'll know in that moment, it's him! He's the one. Your corresponding person."

"My corresponding person? Did you read that in a book? You're too wise for your britches, Prithi. What if Ravi is the love of my life?"

She shrugs wisely. "Then you marry him."

197

Twenty-six

"We are bringing our most sincere congratulations to you and your husband," Auntie Bee says, taking cousin Chandra's hands at the door to her mother's second-floor flat.

"C'mon in and don't track dirt, please," Chandra says. Instead of kneeling to touch the feet of her elder relative, she backs up, holding the door open to let us inside. Nona shuffles in after us, nods to Chandra. Afternoon sunlight slants in through a large bay window. The flat opens into four large rooms connected by archways, similar to Auntie's flat, only the ceilings are higher here, domed and reaching, as if trying to escape Chandra's tight jeans, spray-painted on and then shrink-wrapped. She's an elflike woman, pointy nosed and pointy eared, maybe from Vulcan, her hair like a black shower cap on her head.

Her parents appear from the bedroom as if recently let out of prison. They're traditional, in sari and dhoti punjabi—both pointy nosed and pointy eared too, a family of Indian Vulcans. How can they be related to me?

In the living room, we all sit beneath the lazily spinning ceiling fan. We pick at shortbread biscuits and drink thick, spicy *cha*. The boiled, unpasteurized goat's milk forms a thick film in my cup.

A blond, curly-haired man saunters in, hands thrust into the pockets of his jeans. Unlike Chandra, he erred on the side of baggy. "Hey," he says, waving as if we're miles away.

Chandra's mother, Mrs. Chowdhry, speaks softly in Bengali to the cook, a sweaty, large woman in an orange cotton sari.

"Speak in English, Ma!" Chandra says in a whiny voice and slaps her hand on the coffee table. It's a delicate hand, but the force of the slap makes the table vibrate. Sam, her husband, flops onto the couch next to her.

"Always in English you want me to speak," her mother says, glancing at her father, who shakes his head and focuses on chewing a fifth cookie.

"If you come to New York, you won't be able to talk to everyone in Bengali," Chandra says, slurping her cha. "You'll have to make an effort to fit in, the way I had to do."

"How difficult it is to get about in New York," Mrs. Chowdhry says, addressing us now, an apology in her eyes.

"I learned to call a taxi, but all the time they are rushing by, rushing here and there."

"Taxicabs are the most dangerous form of transportation known to man," Dr. Chowdhry pontificates. He's a university professor, and every sentence comes out a lecture. "They will run you over without mercy. Without looking." He waves his spoon at me.

"When you come to the States next month, don't fill up your suitcase with all those saris," Chandra goes on, speaking to her ma again. Her mother, a meek woman who looks at the ground most of the time, nods.

"She has married this American artist, and already she has lost everything," Dr. Chowdhry says. "Every bit of her mother tongue."

"Sam doesn't understand. It's rude to leave him out." Chandra rubs his back in a provocative way, then his thigh, and they give each other looks fit for a porno movie.

I cringe on behalf of my grandmother and hope her cataracts obscure her view.

"We are hoping you will both come to India for a proper Bengali wedding?" Nona says in her gravelly voice.

"Bengali wedding?" Chandra snorts out through her nose. "But Sam's Catholic. Or at least, his family is. He's gone atheistical on everyone. And who can blame him? Do you know what those Catholic nuns do to kids in those schools? They rap their knuckles. Capital punishment."

"He's an atheist, not atheistical," I say, and it occurs to me that I don't know Nick's religion.

Ma glances at me.

"Whatever." Chandra slurps her tea. "Anyway, we had this really cool eco-friendly wedding out at Rabbit Park north of the city. My friends all brought their bikes to the ceremony and we had a vegan cake."

Part of me admires her for her dedication, and yet I can't warm to my cousin, my blood.

"We were hoping you and Sam would come here for a proper Indian wedding," Auntie Bee says. "All of the family would like to celebrate."

"Are you kidding?" Chandra reaches across the table to grab another cookie. "What a pain in the ass." Nona flinches again. "I mean, we have family all over this damned country. We'd have to invite every single one of them and all their friends, and if we forgot to invite one person, everyone would be in a huff and nobody would talk to us ever again. Not that they talk to us now anyway. But the whole Indian thing, everyone knowing everyone—I can't stand it, don't know how I ever could. In America, you don't have to know anyone if you don't want to."

Chandra's parents droop across the table, their Vulcan ears seeming to fold upon themselves. When we pile into the car to leave, there's a hush, a kind of stunned silence as if we've all been struck by the same bolt of lightning.

"Completely corrupt, that girl," Auntie Bee says. "What's America done to her? Did you see her parents?"

My grandmother shakes her head, clucking her tongue against the roof of her mouth. "We must not speak of others this way."

Auntie Bee, Kolkata's biggest gossip, can't keep her tongue from flying. "She's forgotten bangla, and you see the way she speaks to her mother. Oh-la! I've nearly had a heart attack."

"You'll have one anyway with the heavy yogurt you're eating every morning," Ma says, frowning.

Auntie turns to her and narrows her eyes. "So America has you on exercise and low-cholesterol kicks as well?"

Ma laughs and pats her sister's knee. "Health and exercise are good in any country, Bee. Even here. There are some wonderful things about America—"

"What wonderful? What's Chandra done marrying this strange man with the—hair. Did you hear his tone of voice and attitude?" Auntie says. We're all silent, and I think of Nick.

I clear my throat. "I'm sure he's a good man. You just don't know him yet."

The driver is silent, staring ahead as if he doesn't hear us, as if he's not here.

"Chandra's merely finding her way," my grandmother says, and Auntie purses her lips. "She knows not where she belongs, but she will learn."

Auntie picks at the fingernail of her index finger. "I'm worried about her parents, poor things, always listening to Chandra. And those clothes—those pants. Where do they come from?"

"Auntie," I laugh. "Everyone wears clothes like that in America."

"But we are in India. She is from India. Bangla is her language."

Bengali is my language too, now rusting and derelict in the storage room of my mind, but Ravi brought out the mellifluous language again for me. Isn't language the heart of the homeland, the heart of where we belong?

On the way home I'm sweating, but I'm slowly growing accustomed to the heat. The thick, wet air breathes through me now, becoming one with me.

Marry me.

Sam's atheistical.

No Indian wedding.

Speak in English.

Marry me.

She's lost her culture, that Chandra.

Do you believe in love at first sight?

What decision should I make? Should I fall into Ravi's arms and let the sea of my culture, my destiny, close in around me? Tomorrow we're taking the train north to see Thakurma, my father's mother. Perhaps the answer lies with her.

Twenty-seven

On the train, our carriage car is respectably packed with middle-class travelers. But the rift between rich and poor is so stark here. These women wear expensive silk saris, diamond studs in their noses, and the men wear pressed suits and chat quietly on cell phones.

I sit near the window. Ma has no trouble falling asleep next to me with her chin on her chest. Although she's touching me, no images come through, no trace of the occasional white mountain on which she is standing, her breath rising in wisps of condensing steam. I never know why she's standing there, but the image persists.

The dry dust of Kolkata pollution still coats the inside of my nose, my bronchial tubes all the way to my lungs. The elephant face of the Hindu god Ganesh watches us from doorways, windows, even painted on the front of a photo store called Anjali Cameras. The contours of India, its bustling, compressed culture and chaos, weave tangled webs in my brain.

Eventually, the hills rise in the distance, shrouded by a silvery mist, and the valleys fall away behind us in a mirage of black and blue, tiny rooftops painted on the surface. The train winds up along treacherous cliff edges. We reach the station four hours later, and Ma jolts awake. The air outside must've blown down from the cold, clean side of the moon. Its stark wind shifts over us, bringing the scents of moss and smoke and decaying leaves. The people here have ruddy complexions, clothe themselves in colorful, thick-knit sweaters and tight hats. My teeth chatter as we climb into the rickshaw with our luggage and bounce along the road into town.

Ma pats my leg. Her hand feels warm and radiates contentedness and hope. That's my mother, hanging on to simple thoughts and dreams. Tears glisten at the corners of her eyes. "This is where I used to come with your father, to visit your Thakurdadu and Thakurma, before you were born. Before Thakurdadu died."

The driver whisks us along rocky roads to Thakurma's bungalow. Radha, Thakurma's cook, lets us in. She's in a red cotton sari. She hugs Ma, pinches my cheeks, and says in

Bengali how much she's missed us. She has buck teeth, a ring through her nose, and a wandering left eye, but her voice has a quiet musicality.

The aromas of spices drift in from the kitchen, and someone's descending the stairs slowly, wearing a wrinkled cotton sari, the glasses slipping down her nose. Thakurma! She embraces Ma and me, holding us with tears in her eyes, a glint of my father falling into her face, then disappearing. She ushers us into the living room for tea and biscuits. There are pictures on the walls, ghosts of the past living in the black-and-white worlds long past and silent.

"Ah, Lakshmi—since I last saw you, you've come to resemble your father!" she says. "But a much lovelier version."

"Thank you, Thakurma."

Radha brings us tea.

"Now tell all that you've been doing, all that is not in your letters." Thakurma coughs, takes a slurp of tea.

We talk of insignificant things, the shop, the weather.

"Come, Lakshmi," she says. "I want to show you something." We go upstairs into a bedroom stuck in time, Baba's old room. Every time we come, Thakurma tells us the same story. "This was your Baba's room—when he left for America with you and your ma you were just a baby—I kept his room in case he should return. Guests use it now and then, but essentially it is the same."

I nod and murmur as if seeing the room for the first

time. The bed is made with a woolen spread and a newly washed pillowcase on a flattish pillow. A single bed pushed up against the wall, and through the window, the garden unfolds. There's a cricket bat in the corner, a knit sweater over a chair. A teenage boy's sweater. My father's. A bottle of an English aftershave. A fountain pen on the desk next to a bottle of black ink. And in an old dusty bookshelf, volumes and volumes of books—poetry, fiction, physics—most of them written in Bengali.

Thakurma brings a photo album off the shelf, a book I've never seen before. The spine is cracking. Inside are images of my father as a baby—it must be him—in fading black and white, with a young version of my grandfather pushing him on an old-fashioned bike. Pictures of friends and family members I don't recognize, and as I turn the pages, my father gets older and older, and then there are pictures of him with his college chums, that glint of mischief in his eye. And he's standing with a man who looks like Ravi—Ravi's father! With the Himalayas in the background. And near the back of the book, there's a picture of young Ravi, his father, and my father.

"Your father and Ravi's father, Dilip, were the best of friends," Thakurma says. "They knew each other from when they were little boys. They played horrible jokes on the Ayah—once put a harmless snake in her bed. Sent her off crying until I forced them to apologize. When your

Baba nearly died of typhoid fever, Dilip slept outside his door. From the beginning, God has placed the Gangulis in our path. Dilip married and had a son, Ravi, and your father doted on the child, became his godfather so to speak. . . ."

"Go on, Thakurma."

"Then your father met your ma and you were born. They went to America. By this time, Ravi was nearly six." She pats my knee. "I should love to go abroad again, but I've become much too infirm for such jaunts. My doctor says I'll live a bit longer if I rest, nah?"

I put my arm around her. "Thakurma, don't talk that way. You have many years—"

"Not the case, I'm afraid, Lakshmi. But I'll not stop tending my garden." There's a light of hope in her eyes. Then her gaze catches my necklace. Somehow, the gold ring slipped out and dangles outside my blouse. "What is this?" she whispers, holding the ring close to her face. "The etching—"

A chill goes through me. "Do you recognize it, Thakurma? Nick— The ring turned up when we had the sink fixed in the shop. The ring was stuck in the pipe."

"Yes." Her eyes grow bright. "I know to whom this ring belongs."

My heart races. "How can you know, Thakurma? He— I—found the ring in America."

"This ring belonged to a young woman I once knew," Thakurma says. "Known to our family, in a way. And known to your ma. This woman, Jamila Tarun, went to America. But best not to mention her—"

"Why? Why did she go to America?"

"Best not to speak of such things—you must not wear this ring."

"But Thakurma—I already asked Ma about it."

Her eyes widen. "And what did she say?"

"She told me nothing."

"It is fate that you found this ring, although I wish it had not been so. Wait here." She leaves the room and returns with a small, dog-eared address book. She writes a Bellingham, Washington, address on a slip of paper. "This is where Jamila Tarun lives, last time I knew. Not to mention this, nah?"

I nod, tucking the address into my pocket, my mind full of questions. But Ma's coming up the stairs, standing in the doorway with unbearable sadness in her eyes.

"Now!" Thakurma says with fake joviality. "We shall have a lovely afternoon."

"Yes!" I say, getting up.

"Fate has brought you and Ravi together. When I learned of your match, my heart overflowed."

"We are so glad, Thakurma," Ma says.

"And it is only fitting that the two of you should marry,"

Thakurma goes on. "I pray my heart will last long enough to watch Lakshmi and Ravi exchange garlands."

"Thakurma, we haven't yet . . . I mean, I haven't—"

"I've not had much to live for these past twenty years, but your marriage to Ravi shall bring me great joy."

Twenty-eight

On the train back to Kolkata, I let the scenery roll through me, and I think of the ring and my grandmother. What secret does Jamila Tarun hold? How did her ring fall into the sink? Why should I keep my knowledge of her a secret from my mother? What if Jamila has moved?

And oh, Thakurma, is it true that you've been waiting all this time for my match to Ravi? And yet you're tentative—ephemeral, as if you might dissipate at any moment.

Oh, my grandmother who sends me gifts of gold and silk on my birthdays, whose airmail letters link me to India, who sends pictures of the cousins as they grow older and wiser. Your resonant voice sings in my dreams, and I can't imagine losing you. I remember you as you were when you ruled the family with your eyebrows, still took the stairs two at a time, bunching your sari up in front of your thighs as you climbed. You would never fade, never wane. You were an eternal flame, my faith, but now—

All of this—these terraced gardens giving way to valleys of mustard fields, the vast, dusty sky—reminds me of you. This land of my birth, of Ravi's birth. When I look into his eyes, hear his voice, I know that he is my country, my culture. If I am to stay in America and yet stay Indian, is he not the right person for me?

Okay, Ravi Ganguli, I say to myself. *I will marry you, and we'll see what the future holds.*

Twenty-nine

$\mathcal{M}$y family is giddy, as if they've all been riding a fabulous merry-go-round and jumped off happy and glowing and dizzy. Aunts and uncles and cousins emerge from all corners of the city to congratulate me. Auntie Bee has prepared a huge dinner feast for both Ravi's family and mine.

"You've made a wise decision," Uncle Goola says, taking my hands in his pudgy ones. "I know this has been a difficult time for you, a time of reflection." A few crumbs of pakora stick to the corners of his mouth. He's always carrying remnants of his life, a tea or whisky stain on his shirt, bits of food on his face, dust bunnies caught in his hair. "We've just been speaking with Ravi's parents, and they'll arrange the date of the wedding." Uncle Goola is my de facto father, but I feel a keen hollowness in my chest. My memories of Baba fade around the edges, his face a shadowy blur. Can I remember his voice, the deep rumble that soothed when he sang me to sleep?

"Thank you for taking care of everything, Uncle." I rub his arm affectionately. I watch Ravi move smoothly through the crowd, elegant and handsome in his red kurta and khaki pants, stopping to hold my mother's hands and whisper in her ear, making her laugh. My life carries me on a fast-moving current, and I have nothing to grab onto.

Cousin Meena rushes over and envelops me in a warm hug, then pats my cheeks. Close up, I can see bits of lipstick on her teeth and smell the faint foreign scent of spice and oil. "You're looking pale as every bride-to-be, choto, but let me assure you, this is all normal. I was exactly like you. Nervous and uncertain." She's only a few years older than me, slim and rosy-cheeked, her eyes all aglitter. She points across the room to her husband, a robust man with a beard, glass in hand.

"How did you know it was right?" I ask her.

She stays close, her hand on my arm. "I didn't know. Who ever knows? When I agreed to marry him, I vomited several times and stayed in bed for a week." She takes a deep breath and presses the palm of her hand to her chest. Then she leans in toward me and whispers, "Make sure you wake up before your mother-in-law in the morning—"

"We'll be living in the States. Ravi has a job there." And our bedroom door will have a lock!

"Sooner or later, your mother-in-law will live with you. At first I was getting no sleep, but now all is well."

I think of Rina, the timid woman who came into the shop looking for a sari that wouldn't slip. I won't have to worry about such things.

"I sleep in a nightie," I tell Meena. But will Ravi's mother live with us? If so, will she make unreasonable demands?

Meena goes on, "But now I'm in love, and the most wonderful thing about marriage is that it frees you to discover new things about each other that you couldn't explore before, you know, when the family is always breathing down your neck."

"Our courtship has been rather formal so far," I say. "And short."

"Absolutely normal. You'll have plenty of time."

Ma glows as she flits through the crowd, and when Ravi comes to rest an arm around my shoulders, I'm nearly sure that I can do this. The buoyancy of family will lift my spirits, and I'll float along on their happiness.

"I'll miss you until I can make it to the States," Ravi says. "Just a little while." He grins, the creases forming at the edges of his eyes. I search those eyes, his skin, for a sign of love, and I see the glow of promise. I'll let it come.

"My Lakshmi! Spending too long speaking with the groom!" Ma rushes up, pushing the elegantly embroidered pallu of her sari back up over her shoulder. It's always slipping off. Prithi, Auntie Bee, and several other relatives converge on us.

"The feast should be elaborate," Ma says.

"Roshogollas, jelabis, and sandesh," Prithi says.

"We're not just having desserts all the time," Auntie Bee says. She's curled her hair in tight ringlets all around her head. I brought her a curling iron with an international plug, and I think it has short-circuited the breakers.

"Biryani, fish curry," Ma says. "The wedding must be here, where the family is."

"Of course," I say. Maybe my friends will fly to India.

Tears glisten in her eyes. Her voice comes out low. "Your father would've been so happy—how I wish he were here today." Her thoughts drift to a shadow of my father.

In the night, I lie awake in bed beneath the gauzy mosquito net, the unspoken, invisible lives of my relatives rushing through my head. I try to fold the images and tuck them in neat mental drawers, but they keep bursting out.

Your father would've been so happy.

Is that true, Baba? Why won't you give me a sign?

Nick's face pops into my mind.

That's how I feel about you, Lakshmi.

His kiss.

I dream I'm standing before an Indian priest. He's dressed in a dhoti, reciting mantras, only I'm not wearing a traditional red sari. I'm in a white American bridal gown, Ravi Ganguli standing beside me in traditional Bengali groom's threads—a cream-colored dhoti punjabi inlaid with gold. All around us, the family gathers, their faces glowing.

But the priest recites an American script—*if anyone should object to this marriage, speak now or forever hold your peace,* and there's a man in the doorway, a silhouette advancing toward me. He raises his hand and shouts, but his words are garbled. As he approaches, the butterflies take flight in my stomach. I want to drop everything and run toward him. When I jolt awake in darkness, his presence lingers, as if he's been here, watching me. My body is charged with an erotic awareness, each nerve ending on fire. My fingers grip the bedsheet, and the window stands open, the curtains undulating in rhythm with the breeze. I imagine him climbing in through the window. A breath of damp air blows in, pungent and thick with promise.

"It's only a warning," I say aloud to myself. A cautionary dream, maybe a message from my father. Don't be tempted to fall off the track. You might get stuck in the ditch.

Thirty

$\mathcal{M}$a has arranged my marriage the way she arranges saris—with finesse and attention to detail. Our first day back at the shop is abuzz with the news of my wedding. I'm back in my daytime disguise, glasses, ponytail, and baggy shirt. Ma shows Ravi's photo around, proudly expounds upon our trip to India and to his family. Everyone congratulates me, including customers whose names I've forgotten.

I called to check on Sita the moment I got home. She was still staying with Mitra but had been leaving for long periods during the day. Mitra didn't know where she was going.

I find myself looking to the doorway now, hoping that Sita or Rina or Lillian might stop in, that the next man at the window might be Nick, but he never comes.

In the afternoon, I escape to my desk, a pile of receipts and bills in front of me. I feel shaky and light-headed.

I'm getting married in three months.

"Arranged marriage isn't so bad, is it?" I ask Baba's spirit. "Nobody truly knows a spouse before marriage anyway. You and Ma were an arranged marriage. You grew to love each other, right?" I wonder if, after all these years, he still watches over me. "Tell me I'm doing the right thing." I wait for an answer but hear only voices in the shop and the insistent tap of rain on the roof. "What's the story with Jamila Tarun? What does Thakurma know that I'm not allowed to know?"

Jamila Tarun is not listed in the telephone book, so I send her a short letter and keep her address with the ring in my jewelry box.

Ma speaks to Ravi's parents on the telephone nearly every day, tells every customer about my upcoming nuptials. She keeps a list of family, friends, and distant acquaintances who will receive invitations. Thoughts of Nick begin to fade as Ma and I spend hours looking through the saris, picking light cotton as gifts for the Gangulis' maids and servants, thicker silk for Ravi's relatives.

"Once, horror, my friend gave a cheap cotton sari to the groom's mother," Ma says one afternoon, a pile of saris in front of her. "The mother gave back the sari to the bride after the wedding. 'After wearing heavy silks for so many days,' she said, 'I thought perhaps you would appreciate light cotton.' Can you imagine? Then the mother-in-law even offered to soak the sari, and of course the color ran."

The wedding invitations arrive, written in gold on blue vellum.

"They're beautiful, Ma."

"We have much work to do, sending these."

"Did you have invitations like these when you married Baba?"

"Our invitations were beautiful, gold inlay on parchment." She smiles, but her thoughts betray a poignant sadness, a wisp of something lost.

She perks up when Ravi arrives in the States. He calls to invite me out on the town. "A real date for us, finally!" he says.

When I hang up, I see no bubbles, but I'm filled with anticipation.

I choose a peach chiffon sari that makes my face appear pale and creamy. But I have trouble tying the sari. It keeps slipping down past my petticoat. I opt for a conservative Bengali style, set high to cover my navel.

"Do you want him to think you're a nun?" Ma says. Nuns often teach in schools in India, and they tie their saris in conservative ways.

"Do you prefer that I tie it too low? I'll look filmy!" "Filmy" means I look like a wanton Bollywood actress who shows too much skin.

I opt for somewhere in between, but wearing a sari in the Northwest winter can be a cold proposition. I find a way to fit a black woolen sweater over the sari.

Ma adjusts the pleats, fusses over me and my hair. "Light-colored lipstick for light-colored clothing. And drape the pallu like this—and don't hold the pleats with a hairpin, and no pinning the pallu to your cardigan. You'll look so *Behenji!*"

I haven't heard her say *Behenji* in ages. It's a term used for a would-be sophisticate, a woman eager to look fashionable but who can't tie a sari properly. She might pin her pallu at a clumsy angle.

"Ma, stop fussing—I'll be fine. He won't even notice."

"He'll notice all, especially if you try to look perfect and you mess it up!"

But when Ravi steps across the threshold, all worries vanish. He arrives in a fashionable sports jacket, khaki pants, a blue shirt open at the neck to reveal a tantalizing hint of hair. He takes my hand, his long fingers curled around mine. He kisses my cheek, his lips barely brushing my skin—a promise of our future together.

"You look lovely, Lakshmi."

"Come in, I'm just brushing my hair and I have to put on my shoes." I close the door behind him.

His thoughts are warm, a blanket enveloping me.

"Ah, Ravi, we're delighted!" Ma brings tea to the living

room, the silver tray clattering on the coffee table. Ravi sits on the couch, and I get a flash of Nick sitting there, waiting for me to get a sweater from my room.

I have to forget. I quickly brush my hair, put on my shoes, and sit beside Ravi. A soft vibration moves through him and into me, a matching wavelength of harmony, and Nick disappears.

We exchange the usual pleasantries, Ravi saying that he's settled into his temporary apartment. He's learning his way around the campus and hospital, bought a few things he needs, spoken to his parents. The wedding guests have been invited, the venue arranged in Kolkata.

Then Shiva leaps up onto the table and Ravi gives a start.

"There's another one," I say. "She usually hides."

"I hope she won't do that in our house," he says.

"She might—"

"So, Ravi!" Ma interrupts. "You're to buy a home in the area?" Beneath her excitement, a slight thread of worry wavers.

"We'll be close to you, so Lakshmi can see you nearly every day," he says. "She need not drive. We'll be close to all transportation options."

"But I might want to drive," I say.

"Then you may," Ravi says dismissively. "As you wish." He turns to Ma again. "You are welcome to live with us."

Ma's emotions fall in a tangle of confusion, and a faint

222

face emerges—round, dark, with two hairs on his head, the mountain behind him. "Oh—you are most kind, Ravi," she says. "I couldn't impose."

"We'd worry about you here alone, you see," Ravi says.

I say nothing, swallow the dryness in my throat. Of course Ma could live with us. But—Ravi didn't talk to me about this.

"I can't imagine leaving this house," Ma says. "But perhaps it might be the best thing."

"You need not decide now," Ravi says. "But you are family. All of Lakshmi's family is my family now." A sweet protectiveness emanates from him.

Parvati climbs into my lap. I introduce her to Ravi.

"Ah, Parvati the goddess," Ravi says. He smiles but doesn't touch her.

I think of Nick finding her in the cabinet, carrying her to the floor.

"She likes to hide," I say. "Mainly in the cabinet above the refrigerator."

"What a strange thing to do. As long as she doesn't do this in our new home." Ravi chuckles, and Ma hastily rearranges her sari. A funny taste comes into my mouth.

"She might do that sometimes," I say. "She likes to sleep on towels in the linen closet too—"

"Oh, so, Ravi!" Ma exclaims. "How is the new job?" Her teacup clatters onto the saucer.

"Good enough to allow me to take Lakshmi to the finest restaurant." He gets up. "Shall we go?"

His car, a Toyota Camry, is spotless, not a CD or speck of dust on the seat. The scents of air freshener and his spicy cologne permeate the air.

"Where are we going?" I ask.

"We can't settle for mediocre food. Life is too short," he says as he drives away from the curb. He's a careful driver, but I find I'm gripping the armrest, unsure if he's looking both ways when he crosses an intersection.

"We're going to the India Pavilion," he says, slipping a CD into the stereo. The soft strains of a Mozart concerto fill the car. "Four stars in the *Times*. Five stars for atmosphere, four for the food. Moderately priced."

"You've done your research!"

"I had quite a time choosing between this one and the Mayuri, although that one seemed like a bit of a drive. I checked the routes and mileage and concluded that India Pavilion was our best bet."

"You're so . . . thorough." I lean back against the headrest, surprised at the fatigue in my bones. I want to close my eyes and drift into sleep.

"The critics know what they're talking about, especially that Romeo Malliutt, the one who reviews the ethnic restaurants for the *Gazette*."

"You're settling into life here quickly."

"I remember this city—lovely, but a bit cold and damp."

With Nick, I barely noticed the weather.

"But what if the critic has bad taste?" I ask. "What if you disagree with him? I mean, he could prefer mangoes to cantaloupe, and you might prefer cantaloupe."

Ravi laughs, an easy, refined sound. "A good critic takes into account the differences in taste."

"How can he account for differences? I mean, taste is subjective."

"He can tell if food is too greasy, tasteless, not presented in a proper way."

"I guess you're right." I close my eyes, the sound of the road outside distant and insubstantial.

At the restaurant, he's made a reservation at a quiet corner table, away from the cold air coming through the door. There's a view across the water.

"My parents are looking forward to the ceremony." He steeples his fingers in front of him, elbows on the tablecloth. "As am I."

"I'm looking forward to it too," I say, but the tingle of anticipation inside my stomach could be anxiety.

"Have you sent the invitations to your side of the family?"

"We were going to consult you and your family first."

"I think we should invite everyone so as not to offend anyone," he says.

"But the list could get bigger and bigger," I say, thinking of Ma's friends and relatives.

"Then let it—half the people won't come anyway," he says. "Ma's making up our list. I can't remember all these things."

"Your ma's meticulous," I say.

"Very well organized. She understands the nuances."

We peruse the menu, standard North Indian fare with some South Indian vegetarian curries thrown in. I order sparkling water, and Ravi orders an expensive Merlot. Is he planning to drink and drive? Nick didn't drink alcohol the whole time we were together. He knew he would have to drive. There's nothing wrong with a single glass of wine, is there? I have to stop thinking about Nick.

When we get our drinks, Ravi makes a toast. "To our wedding," and the glasses clink together in delicate unison.

We order a variety of the restaurant's starred, recommended dishes. He takes my hands in his, stares into my eyes. "I think we should marry sooner. I wanted to tell you at my parents', but I didn't want to spring it on you at the last minute."

My heart turns upside down. "Soon? But how soon?"

"A month sooner."

"But the planning. Two months! We won't be able to—"

"We'll make it work. My ma will make it work. What do you think, Lakshmi? You look pensive."

Why am I so restless?

"Of course. That will be fine."

I can't imagine life beyond the ceremony. Perhaps I'm not meant to imagine the future. I'll have to share a bedroom with him. My mind travels away, and at night, when I dream, I'm walking beside Nick. A spark turns to fire inside me, and when I wake up, I'm sweating.

Thirty-one

The next afternoon, Sita stops by the store. She's wearing a turquoise sari. Her cheeks are pink, and there's a bandage across the top of her forehead.

"Sita!" I give her a hug. "I tried calling for you—"

"I know. I haven't been at Mitra's lately."

"You look lovely. But what's happened to your head?"

"Just a scrape! Long story. I came to say good-bye and thank you. The orange chiffon sari you gave me did wonders." She glances with affection around the store.

"Ah yes—the orange. It felt right to me."

"It was. And I've got a job. A good one, but not here. In Bangalore."

I drop the sari I'm holding, quickly pick it up. "Congratulations! But . . . you're moving to India?"

"With Kishor. He's waiting in the car."

"But Sita—"

"I couldn't let my family down," she says. "I missed my ma, my sisters."

"But—"

"The sari you gave me, it was slippery."

"Now I remember."

"It always unraveled—got caught in the car door, and I tripped and hit my head—"

"Oh, no!"

"Not to worry—it was for the good. The hospital called my parents, and my ma and Baba came rushing over. Faced with the prospect of losing her only daughter, my ma came around."

"What do you mean, she came around?"

Sita bites her lip, then smiles. "My ma has always been loud, you know. But her bark is much worse than her bite. She is hard on the outside, but inside, she has always loved me. She said as much. We had a long chat in the hospital. She broke down and cried. She said I don't have to marry Kishor if I don't want to, that we could talk. Just knowing that she is on my side, that she will support me, is so gratifying, Lakshmi, and so rare in a family, you know?"

"Wow—I'm so glad." I hug her again. "Not about you hitting your head, though!"

"Kishor came to see me in the hospital too. He stayed with me, held my hand. He was so tender, Lakshmi. You can't imagine! I think I fell in love with him at that moment. I'm happy now. Thank you for everything you've done for me. I couldn't have known how I felt about Kishor until I left him. Until he rallied to come to my side. I couldn't have reconciled with Ma if it weren't for the unraveling sari."

"I'm glad I could help. Be good, okay? And if you ever need anything—"

"I know, just call." She kisses me on the cheek. "You are like a sister to me."

"And you're the little sister I never had."

"I'll write," she shouts back over her shoulder as she rushes outside.

Sita's happy again, back with her family. I never would've guessed. I never would've known that the slippery sari would help her reconcile with her mother, but the sari could just as easily have killed her. Saris bring happiness and love, but they can also be dangerous. How many saris have been caught in car doors, in escalators? Burst into flames over a stove? How many bride burnings have been attributed to saris *accidentally* catching fire?

One never knows which way the wind will shift.

Thirty-two

$\mathcal{M}$itra picks me up for lunch on Thursday, but this time, she's quiet on the drive to the café.

"Thanks for taking care of Sita," I tell her. "I'm so glad she's happy again."

"She really loves Kishor. She's willing to give it a go." Mitra sighs. "I met him. He's a great guy! Eager to please her. And he stands up to her mother. Can you imagine?"

"Wow—good for him!"

"He's a godsend for Sita. He'll be a good husband to her. He won't let her mother walk all over her. Maybe I ought to look into an arranged marriage. Now that my father . . . Anyway, he's coming to my performance Saturday. I'm going to wear that costume."

"Good for you!"

"Maybe I want a guy like Kishor. Handsome and loving. Not like Nisha's . . ." Her voice trails off.

"What about Nisha?"

"She's unhappy." Mitra parks at the café and stares out through the windshield, which is streaked with rain.

"I know—I sensed that the last time we had lunch here. She was running to an apartment building, but I didn't want to say anything. She's a very private person."

"Maybe she just had a bad childhood memory."

"Maybe. Well, now she and Rakesh are happy together." But a shiver of apprehension climbs my spine.

"Don't push her. You know how proud she is." Mitra gives me a warning look.

When we go inside, Nisha's dressed perfectly as usual, her copper-colored suit jacket falling elegantly across her shoulders.

"Congratulations!" she tells me. "I hear you're marrying a perfect gentleman."

"Thanks, Nisha—but I was hoping for a man like Rakesh." I wink at her.

She gives me a wan smile, while Mitra chatters about her dancing, her dates, her new power juicer, which makes perfect fruit punches. All the talking masks an undercurrent of darkness. Her father is even frailer now, coughing all the time.

The image of Nisha barges in. She's running in a tattered green sari. She arrives at an apartment complex, takes the concrete stairs two at a time to a door. The full moon is a big yellow disk in the sky. She stops, her hand on the knob. Her fingers, smooth and covered in silver rings, look white in the moonlight.

She enters a dim, starkly furnished apartment. Walks to a bedroom.

"Nisha, pass the salt!" Mitra says. She's chattering about the way Sita brushed her teeth all the time and cooked Indian food in Mitra's kitchen. "Left turmeric stains all over the counter," Mitra says.

Nisha's nodding, while the images keep coming. She's at the bedroom door. Inside, a man sits up in the bed. He's naked, with a slight belly but a handsome face, hair sticking up in places, a sheen of sweat on his body. Rakesh!

No, no. Nisha, turn away!

But she doesn't.

A pillow has fallen to the floor, and there's a clock ticking on the bedside table. She's aware of the sound growing louder, not changing its rhythm while her heart races ahead. The woman next to Rakesh sits up slowly, as if she's been asleep.

Nisha's reaction startles her—the first thought should be, *How could he do this?* But instead, she thinks, *She's not even beautiful.* The woman's too thin, all bones, her skin too dark.

Rakesh is yelling—*Nisha. What are you doing here? Why didn't you stay home?* As if all this, what she's seeing, is actually her fault. She backs away, the heartbeat flooding her head, flooding mine, and then she lets go of me, and the image wrenches away.

"What's going on?" Mitra's hand is on mine.

Nisha's holding a fork halfway to her mouth. Her fingers tremble.

"It's Rakesh," I whisper to Mitra.

Nisha glances from Mitra to me and back. Her eyes grow bright. She drops the fork on her plate.

"I'm so sorry." I jump up and hug Nisha. I don't care how formal she is. I don't care if she's put up a wall. "Nisha. We're your friends. We love you."

She lets me hug her, and her bony shoulders begin to shake.

"What the hell is going on?" Mitra asks. "Is this a group hug?" She comes over and hugs both of us.

"You have to leave him," I tell Nisha.

"I know," she sobs. "I did."

The waiter comes with drink refills, and we all sit down again. I keep my hand over Nisha's. Tears roll down her cheeks.

"You left Rakesh?" Mitra screeches.

My two best buddies are the only two who understand the true nature of the *knowing*.

"I saw him with the other woman," I tell her.

"Which one?" Nisha whispers.

The blood drains from my face. "Oh, Nisha."

"Oh, no!" Mitra rolls her eyes. "Rakesh is a player. I knew it! Nisha, you deserve better."

"I didn't know," Nisha says. "Over a couple of years, he charmed me. And I let down my guard. He came from a good family, had a good job. After our wedding, he started leaving on long business trips, and even when he was in town, he'd stay at 'work' all night. One night, I decided to follow him." She wipes the tears from her cheeks.

"Oh, honey." Mitra hugs her again.

"I was lucky he agreed to a divorce," Nisha says.

"Why didn't you tell us?" I ask.

"I couldn't. It was a dream—I wanted to hold onto it, but I had to let it go. I moved back into my parents' house a couple of days ago. It all happened so quickly. I think I'm going back to school."

I sense a glimmer behind her grief, and I glimpse an imperial violet muslin fabric. On the top shelf in the shop.

"I have a sari that might help you through this," I tell her.

"I knew you would." She smiles at me, and a bit of color returns to her cheeks. I've given her something she didn't have a few minutes ago. Something humans can never live without. Hope.

Thirty-three

That afternoon, I receive a letter addressed to me in shaky script, with no return address.

> Dear Ms. Sen,
>   I was surprised to receive your note some time ago. I've never forgotten the ring. Please do come and see me this Sunday afternoon, if you can manage.
>
>   Yours,
>   Jamila Tarun

Jamila Tarun!
Invisible secrets run between the lines, and my heart

pounds. There's something about Jamila Tarun, and something else crazy, a promise I made to Nick. I would let him know when I found the ring's owner.

Finder's keepers.

I take his business card from my jewelry box, and our moments together rush back to me as if they happened yesterday. They're supposed to fade with time, not grow stronger.

My fingers tremble as I punch his number into the phone. He answers immediately, his voice melting my bones.

"Nick? This is Lakshmi."

"Hi, Lakshmi."

"I, uh, found the owner of the ring. An old friend of the family. She wants me to visit."

"Yeah?"

Ma pops her head into my bedroom. "Bibu, who are you talking to?"

"A friend." I make a cross face at her, my heart pounding, and she disappears.

I lower my voice. "My grandmother told me that nobody should know about this Jamila—I don't know why. I'm wondering if you could take me to see her. I'm hiring you, as a driver!"

"When?"

"Next Sunday afternoon. I'll be waiting at the corner."

*   *   *

Nick arrives in jeans and a black jacket over a blue turtle-neck, accentuating the pure blue of his eyes. He strides around to open my door, and my heart leaps. I have a crazy urge to jump into his arms.

"I've missed you," I breathe as I get into the car.

He gets into his side and starts the engine. "Directions?"

So, he's going to be formal.

I give him the address.

He pulls out into the road, looking straight ahead.

"Nick—how have you been?"

"Great. You?"

"I went to India."

"I know."

"Thanks for doing this—if I'd told anyone else, they would've blabbed to my mother."

"No problem." His sheer size and presence overwhelm me. My throat is dry. A few stray, fuzzy bubbles hover in the air, then tiny white flowers appear—haloes of baby's breath.

"Nick, I—"

"Asha told me you're getting married. She heard from a customer she knows. Congratulations."

"Thanks. How are her wedding plans going?"

"She's having some fabrics sent from India and she's planning to have a tailor make the clothes."

"But so little time is left until her wedding!"

"She keeps her own counsel."

We don't speak the rest of the way. The baby's breath slowly wilts on the seat between us.

Jamila's home is a large cedar-sided complex with an A-frame roof and skylights.

"It's an assisted-care facility," I say. "The Cedars. I thought that was the name of her street!"

He gets out and strides to my side, then he opens the door and unclasps the seat belt. "You want me to go in with you?"

I look into his eyes, where I find some strange safety. "Yes, can you come?"

We get out and sign in at the front desk, a pleasant, spacious room with a pink carpet and leafy indoor plants. The woman at the desk is young. Elderly people pass in the halls, some pushing walkers, a couple in wheelchairs. Nick leads me down two hallways. He knocks, and a faint voice calls from inside. "Come in!"

Mrs. Tarun lives in a large studio apartment, her hospital bed against a wall. The room fills with the acrid odor of disinfectant.

"Do come in and sit!" she calls in a thin voice.

I instinctively take Nick's hand. Why am I nervous? Mrs. Tarun's a wisp of a woman in bed, her black hair shot through with streaks of gray. She's perhaps my mother's age, but she's frail, wasted by some mysterious disease.

"You must be Lakshmi," she says. "Please do sit, sit—my hearing isn't too good. The illness, you know. So please speak up."

"Mrs. Tarun," Nick says in a loud, firm voice. "It's stuffy in here. I'll open the window."

"Oh, you're such a honey, and such a handsome young man. Please do open that window. I've been trying to get that nurse in here, but she must've taken another cigarette break."

Nick steps around the bed and yanks open the window, letting in cool, fresh air.

I sit in the chair next to the bed.

"What a lovely husband you have," Mrs. Tarun says to me. "How long have you two been married?"

"We're not married," I say.

"Newlyweds then? You make a perfect couple, so good together. I can see the two of you are very happy. Any children yet?"

"No kids yet." Nick helps her sit up against the pillows.

She strains to see out the window. "Well then you two ought to have children. And you'll have such fun trying, won't you?"

Nick looks at me, and I blush.

"We're not married, Mrs. Tarun," I say again, avoiding Nick's gaze.

"What, honey? You're on my bad side. I'm completely deaf in my left ear."

"She says, we're having fun trying," Nick shouts, and Mrs. Tarun smiles.

I hand her the ring. She holds it up to the light, and tears spill from her eyes. Nick is standing motionless, only the twitch of his lip betraying emotion.

"Thank you for this," she says. "I will treasure it. And how is your mother?"

"Ma's well," I say.

She's silent. "Tell her I asked after her."

"I will. She sends her best."

"You're lying—your ma would not have let you come here, that much is certain."

I pull the chair up close to her. "Why? What's the story behind that ring, Mrs. Tarun?"

She wipes her eyes. "It was a long time ago. You don't need to know, my dear."

"How did it end up in the pipes?"

"I was in anguish, and your mother was . . . well, angry." She falls silent, staring at the wall.

"Mrs. Tarun. Please tell me."

"You see, I knew your father before he met your mother."

"You were friends?"

"We went to university together for a while . . ."

"And?" My heart races.

"Oh, Lakshmi. How beautiful you've become. I'm sure

you don't remember me, but when I came to the store, you were still tiny, but you already knew which saris would help people. You pointed out the chiffon that saved my life."

Nick shoves his hands in his pockets and stares out the window.

"I don't remember, Mrs. Tarun. I don't remember you, either. I'm sorry."

"Of course—I left the store bereft, certain that my life would end. But the sari saved me. It was most delightful, cloudy chiffon, quite slimming. I wore it to a dance, and that's where I met my husband."

"You're married?"

"I was—he died two years back. We have two boys who visit me every day. They wanted me to live with them, but I don't want to be a burden, you see. They have families."

Nick pipes up. "You wouldn't be a burden to anyone, Mrs. Tarun."

"Oh, you're so kind, young man." Her face brightens. "Can you prop me up higher, my dear boy?"

Nick props her up as high as she can go. "Is that better?"

"I wish I could see out that window, but I can't see a thing. That nurse is going to have to move my bed—"

Nick makes as if to move the bed.

"Oh, no, no, young man! I could get into big trouble for moving the furniture—not supposed to."

Nick does something unexpected then—he tucks the

blanket underneath her legs and lifts her bodily. She's a mere thought in his arms. She lets out a thin exclamation as he carries her to the window. "There, Mrs. Tarun. You can see out from here."

"Oh, young man! If you weren't married to that lovely young lady, I'd ask you to marry me!"

"And I would gladly do so." He holds her there at the window, in his arms, and my heart fills. She smiles out at the lake, dotted with boat sails, the scenery lit by the afternoon sun.

Thirty-four

On the way home, there's a lump in my throat, and when I finally speak, my voice comes out hoarse. "You were very good with Mrs. Tarun."

"Everyone has grandparents," Nick says.

"But not everyone carries them to the window."

"She couldn't get there herself."

"She wouldn't tell me the story of the ring," I say. "Why do you think that is?"

"I think you already know the story," Nick says. "Your intuition is always with you. What does it tell you now?"

"The ring made her sad. She knew my father. She came to see my mother. They haven't seen each other in years. They fought."

Nick drums his fingers on the steering wheel at the stop-light. Then I hear the cell phone ring in his pocket. He flips open the phone. "Liz—yeah, dinner. I'll pick you up at seven." He hangs up and tucks the phone into his pocket as the light changes to green.

My heart falls into my sandals. "Liz? You're seeing her."

"On and off."

I cross my arms over my chest. "Boy, you move quickly."

"So do you, Ms. Indian princess. I'm not the one en-gaged."

"Touché. So . . . do you tell her that it's love at first sight, because—"

"No."

"I know. It's none of my business—"

"Lakshmi, you're engaged."

When he stops in front of my house, my legs feel leaden, but Nick's already out, opening my door.

"Good-bye, Lakshmi," he says, and leaves.

The tears press at the backs of my eyes. I take a deep breath, preparing to talk to my mother.

When I tell her where I've been, Ma's face goes pale. She's on the couch, a catalog open on her lap. Only upon second look, I see it's not a catalog but a travel brochure, showing pictures of mountains.

"Baba loved another woman when he married you." My voice wavers on a high wire.

ANJALI BANERJEE

"Your Baba loved me dearly," she says.

I pace. "I know he did, Ma. But he was in love with Jamila, wasn't he?"

Ma startles, just the tiniest tremor of her fingertips. "Young men do silly things."

"She came here to find him, didn't she?" My voice is a helium balloon rising into the atmosphere.

Ma doesn't reply, her tremor of sadness a black thread.

"Did they have an affair, Ma?"

Her gaze shifts to me again, and she gives me a weak smile. "Only before we were married, Bibu. When Jamila came to the shop looking for him, he was already gone."

I deflate on the couch. My eyelids feel heavy. "And that's why she was sad? Because she came looking for him and discovered that he was already . . . dead?"

Ma nods, sadness falling into her shoulders. "You see, Bibu, your father gave her the ring before he married me. And then . . . his parents introduced us, and we were married."

"You didn't marry for love." But I knew that.

Did he love Jamila for the rest of his life?

"Ah, Bibu, these things are better left unspoken."

"Why, Ma? Why not talk about them? Did Baba ever love you?" Everything I believed, all my quaint thoughts about my childhood, begin to crumble.

"Of course he loved me," she says. "And he loved you too."

"But he was in love with Jamila. When he went to India, did he see her?" My voice is thin and tight.

"I don't know." Ma looks down at her hands. We may never know, I realize.

"And do you love Mr. Basu?"

Ma gives me a sharp look. "What are you saying?"

"I thought maybe he was taking advantage of you, but—"

"He is not taking advantage," she says quietly.

"Ma—why didn't you tell me?"

She closes the travel brochure. Himalayas, it reads. "I did not want to trouble you. I thought that perhaps, with your increased sensitivity, you might draw your own conclusions."

"I didn't understand about you and Mr. Basu, not at first."

"Perhaps you see what you want to see sometimes, Bibu."

"Still, you didn't have to hide—"

"What would people have said? You were not yet matched—"

"What does my match matter, Ma? Why Mr. Basu?"

"He is kind, and attentive to me. We have fun together. He takes good care of me. He may not look it, but he's a considerate man."

"Have you been seeing him a long time? I thought that one time—"

"What time?"

"I thought that one weekend you spent with him—"

"There were many weekends, Bibu. You've always been so stuck on Baba. Damaged by his death. You were so young. I did not want to hurt you."

"Damaged? What do you mean, damaged?"

"Let your Baba go, Lakshmi."

Me, let him go? She's the one who needs to let him go! *Always take care of your mother.*

I stomp off to my room, and that night, my father returns to my dreams. We're standing in a misted forest, the air cool and refreshing. He's wearing a woolen coat, perhaps the one he wore to Darjeeling. His face remains obscured in shadow. He shoves his hands into his pockets, hunches against the cold. His breath comes out in puffs of steam. "My dearest child," he says. "You know I have always loved you."

A lump comes up in my throat. Then why did you leave? I want to say, but I'm speechless.

"I didn't leave you purposely," he says. "These things happen. Planes crash, trains derail. Flesh and blood can't fight these twists of fate."

I know this is true, that accidents and tsunamis and earthquakes happen, that the planets move in mysterious ways. "But aren't Ravi and I lucky to have found each other?" I ask in desperation.

My father paces, leans his shoulder against a tree. The mist is a living thing, creeping in around our feet. "Not a coincidence. Your mother knew where to find him. She was just waiting for the right time."

"I think I knew that, Baba. But still—"

"There are other things in life that happen by accident. Someone walks in front of you, smiles at you in the street. Serendipity."

"Baba—what are you trying to say?"

Now he steps into the light, and his face is young but distant, washed in sepia, shaded by age and regret. A face kept young for too long. "I am trying to say that it happened to me."

"Someone walked in front of you, smiled at you in the street?"

"Before I knew your mother."

Words strangled in my throat. "You loved Ma, didn't you?"

"The way one grows to love one's home." His voice drips with sadness.

"Like a rug or a sagging armchair?" I shout. "Or like true love?"

"I loved—*love* you more than anything," he says. "My Bibu."

"Baba—you didn't answer my question." But already I know the answer.

I run toward him, but with every step, he moves farther away. The mist fades, and then I'm awake, in the world of the living.

Thirty-five

*T*he next morning, I corner Mr. Basu in the office before anyone else arrives. He's got a pile of new saris around him.

"Do you love my mother?" I ask him, hands on my hips.

"What?" He glances up at me, the two hairs standing straight up on his head. But his face looks different today, not quite as round. He's drinking a double-tall mocha. I didn't know he drank coffee.

"You've been sleeping with my mother. Do you love her?"

He stands, and suddenly he looks taller than usual. "Do you love Ravi Ganguli?"

I sputter, no words coming out.

"Lakshmi," he says quietly. "I wondered when you would come to talk to me."

"What do you mean, when?"

"You are always trying so hard to take care of your mother."

"What do you mean, trying so hard? What do you know?"

"Your ma and I are very happy. You can let go."

"Let go of what? I'm not holding onto anything!"

He takes a long sip of his mocha. "I knew your ma in India, before I lost my hair. Before I had this paunch." He pats his belly, which doesn't look quite as big today. "You are probably wondering how she could love a man like me."

"No, that's not what I meant—"

"Perhaps she loved me long ago, Lakshmi. Before she met your father. Your ma and I, we laughed together, we hiked, we went to the cinema."

"Mr. Basu—"

"When she sees me now, she doesn't see my paunch. She sees me the way I was. I am still a young man in here." He points to his bald temple. I catch a glimpse of him as a young man, slim and—handsome! "But you don't see, Lakshmi. You see what you want to see."

"I see perfectly well!"

Mr. Basu comes up to me and searches my eyes. So close, I'm surprised to find that he's actually a little taller than me. "Find your happiness, Lakshmi. Your mother has found hers. Let us be together. You must trust. I will take care of her."

I squeeze Mr. Basu's hands. I can hardly speak for the catch in my throat. "You'd better be good to her."

And then Ma and Pooja arrive, and we're lost in the bustle of morning activity. Just before noon, a gangly boy comes into the shop and walks around, looking embarrassed. He's familiar to me—oh! He's Anu, the boy who came to buy a sari for his mother, the first time I met Nick. When the *knowing* disappeared.

This teenager must be here to tell me I ruined his relationship with his mother. The *knowing* slipped away, and he took home a blue sari that made her look frumpy. She must've thrown the sari out in the street.

Anu spots me, waves, and rushes over. "Ms. Lakshmi," he says in a serious voice.

There's no escape. "I'm so sorry, I don't know what came over me that day. If you need to return the sari, please do—"

"No, no! The sari was perfect!"

"What do you mean, perfect?"

"When I gave it to Ma, she cried. She said she had been looking for a midnight blue sari all her life. The way the colors changed in the light, she said, was a dream!"

"A dream?"

"She said it was as if you had reached into her head and pulled out all her thoughts and wishes."

But the *knowing* was gone. Nick had taken it away.

Just then a beautiful woman glides into the shop. She's tall, angular, her skin smooth and milky, only the hint of creases around her eyes belying her age. She's wearing the midnight blue sari, a matching blouse, and holding the pallu over her arm in an elegant style. "This sari has brought me great happiness, and I must thank you myself," she says. "My son and I will come in here more often now."

"Of course, I can help you!" I spend the next half hour picking out sari after sari. After Anu and his mother leave, I escape to the office to catch my breath. I picked the right sari while the bubbles hovered around my head. A glimpse of the *knowing* must've peered through.

Intuition, Nick said. *You always have it.*

I think of him carrying Mrs. Tarun to the window, his tenderness. *Do you believe in love at first sight?*

You two make a lovely couple, Mrs. Tarun said.

Did she love my father all her life? She said the chiffon sari saved her life. She found the man she would marry, but did she love him? Was she happy? Did she compromise?

Did Ma always love Mr. Basu?

You must trust. I will take care of her.

Baba—maybe Mr. Basu is right. Maybe I can let go.

Ma comes rushing through the store, carrying a taped package from India. "I ordered this some time ago, Lakshmi, and it has finally arrived! Heavy red silk inlaid with gold! Your wedding sari!"

Thirty-six

I take the sari home. In my room, I change into a petti-coat and red blouse and stand in front of the full-length mirror. I'm nearly fully clothed, but in India, I would feel naked without the sari.

I hold the wedding sari up to my chest. A concentrated inner light shimmers from the red silk. The fabric breathes, as if the fibers are alive. A faint, indefinable scent rises from the intricate gold weave—a mixture of newness and ancient India. In the folds, I see the future of a family, a bride smiling through a translucent pallu. The sari changes texture and color to become all the saris she will ever own—soft cottons, georgette, silk, chiffon. She uses the sari to dab the sweat from her brow, to shield her head in the sun, to wipe her daughter's tears. A small boy grips his mother's pallu, takes his first tentative steps. Her husband will slowly unravel the sari in a soft dance of foreplay. She will cover her mouth in a coy gesture as she runs from him. Will the sari get caught in a door, accidentally fall off at an embarrassing moment?

I have to try on this wedding sari, but my fingers won't move. The garment grows heavy in my hands, and when I unfold the fabric, it slips through my fingers. It's worth several thousand rupees, one of a kind, handwoven in a natural, heavy silk with the finest embroidery, and yet I can't put it on. I just stand there looking at it.

Thirty-seven

Saturday morning, Mrs. Dasgupta shows up rosy-cheeked, looking much younger than her seventy years. "The blue sari you gave me has brought me great happiness, Lakshmi." She pats my cheek, shows me an airmail letter. "I sent my dear friend Adith a snap of me in that sari, and he wrote back immediately, told me I resembled Sridevi from *Mr. India*!"

"How risqué of him!" I give her a warm smile. It's hard to imagine Mrs. Dasgupta as Sridevi, the voluptuous and beautiful actress who writhes in an erotic, wet sari scene in the classic Hindi movie—but the sari must've done wonders.

Mrs. Dasgupta lowers her voice. "The way the thing clings, you know—made me look many years younger."

"Who is this Adith?" I ask, but I already know. The shadow-man in her mind, the man who stood in the background all these years, behind the groom who is now long dead. Adith steps into the light. He has a soft face, kind eyes, a handlebar mustache. He's been waiting.

"He's coming to visit me," she says. "Perhaps to stay. He's a widower now. And you helped me find him. All with that sari. Your saris are sacred, I tell you. How did you know? You always see what it is I am thinking."

"I didn't see. I only guessed. It is a mystery. Everything's a mystery, especially love, right?"

She gives me a funny look. "Love?" She purses her lips.

Yes, love, Mrs. Dasgupta. I pat her hand. "I'm very happy for you."

"And I am happy for you." She pats my cheek with the sandpaper palm of her hand, her filmy eyes examining every crease of my skin. "But something troubles you, Lakshmi. Not getting cold feet, are you?"

"No cold feet." Icicle feet. Stone feet.

And that's when the door swings open and I don't have to look to know. Asha is here. Nick is pushing her in the wheelchair. The saris whisper his name, the black suit moving in perfect harmony with his body. A body I could picture with my eyes closed.

Asha's in a fashionable lemon chiffon sari today, silver threads crisscrossing the centerpiece, an elaborate silver pattern on the pallu. She has the glowing look of a woman in love.

Ma moves forward in slow motion, her pencil-thin eyebrows rising in surprise. She doesn't know why Asha is here, doesn't know that I called her.

I wasn't sure she would come.

The *knowing* spirals away, but this time, I understand that it's not truly gone. It has merely changed shape. I still have a *knowing* inside me, a deeper kind of intuition borne of being human, of simply being me, a woman of compassion. Perhaps this is all it ever was—part of me.

"What is this—Asha Rao again?" Mrs. Dasgupta whispers. "Oh, Shiva, what I'll tell my friends!"

"Ms. Rao, what a pleasure!" Ma exclaims, and Mr. Basu is running after her, always her faithful follower.

"How can we help you?" he says. "We've got new shipments, many lovely new—"

"Lakshmi called, said it was urgent," Asha says.

"Lakshmi called?" Ma says and gives me a look full of questions.

"Oh, Shiva." Mrs. Dasgupta's lashes flutter.

"Bibu, what's going on?" Ma asks in a sharp voice.

Pooja rushes out of the office, her eyes wide, hair frizzy. She's a bundle of angles in a green shalwar kameez. "Oh, my!" she exclaims. "Nick! Asha!"

I turn to Nick, who's staring at me with a touch of sadness in his eyes.

Mrs. Dasgupta stands like a statue, gazing in utter awe at Asha Rao.

Mr. Basu coughs, and the two hairs droop, portending a storm. "We can clothe all of you, of course, if that's the plan—"

"Sanjay!" Ma shouts. She puts her hands on her hips. "Lakshmi, explain."

"I have an announcement to make," I say.

"What is this?" Ma says.

"I have the perfect wedding sari for Asha."

"I've already chosen a wedding sari," Asha says quietly. "And besides, the last time you showed me a sari—"

"Forget the last time," I say. "This one is perfect."

"But I've already—"

"Please, give me a chance."

Asha points toward the door. "Nick, turn me around. We're leaving. This woman has ruined my looks once in a lifetime, and it won't happen again."

"No, it won't," I say. "Nick, don't you turn around!"

He hesitates. Yes, I can raise my voice.

"Lakshmi!" Ma says. "You don't talk to customers that way."

Mrs. Dasgupta presses a hand to her chest and whispers to me, "Do you think Asha would give me her autograph?"

"Just wait!" I bring out a paper bag and unfold my wedding sari in front of Asha. The silk's inner light radiates through the shop. The fabric breathes stories of the past and future. Asha's mouth drops open. She reaches for the sari, her fingers trembling.

"Lakshmi!" Ma's scream rips the silence. "That is your wedding sari!"

Asha withdraws her hand and snaps her head around to glare at me. "Is this true? This is your wedding sari? What kind of joke are you playing here?"

"It's not a joke. My mother's right. It is my wedding sari, but I'm not keeping it."

Ma gasps. "What do you mean, you're not keeping it? There is no other sari like this one anywhere in the world."

"Exactly, Ma. No other sari like this one, and it's perfect for Asha." I can feel Nick's regard, but he keeps his expression carefully blank.

Asha bites her lip in a delicate gesture, a glimmer of hope in her eyes. "This is most . . . amazing."

"Oh, no! What is happening here?" Ma presses her hands to her cheeks. Mr. Basu rushes over and wraps his arms around her, and she collapses against him, forgetting for the moment that she's supposed to be constantly irritated with him.

"I'm sorry, Ma," I say. "I wanted to tell you, but you never would've let me do this."

"Oh, Bibu. You have not tried the wedding sari? It's the sari for you." She leans against Mr. Basu, who proves to be surprisingly strong for his size.

"I'm not going to wear it, Ma. I couldn't wear it."

Nick's silent, watching me.

Asha presses the sari to her cheek, sniffs the fabric, holds it up to her chest, runs her fingers along the fine gold trim. "It's absolutely—beautiful," she breathes. "Amazing. I've never seen a sari like this one."

"And you never will again," I say.

"I can't let go of it."

"Oh, Shiva," Mrs. Dasgupta whispers.

"It's perfect," Asha says. "How did you know, Lakshmi?"

"I thought of you in it, and I knew it was yours."

Mr. Basu fans Ma's face, although the store is cool.

"Oh, Bibu, why have you done this?" Ma says. "What are we to do? How will we find you a better sari?"

"We won't," I say, "because I'm not getting married."

"What!" Ma shrieks. She elbows her way out of Mr. Basu's arms. "What is this nonsense? Lakshmi Sen—"

"Just what I said, Ma. I can't get married to Ravi. He's a good man, the right match, but—"

"You've gone crazy!" Ma says.

"Let her speak," Pooja says, eyes wide. I expect her to pull up a chair and grab a bag of popcorn.

Nick's gaze burns through me.

"Ravi's a wonderful man, but I don't love him."

"You don't love him," Ma says in a flat, faraway voice.

"No, Ma, I don't. If I loved him, I would marry him."

Ma stands straight, finding her strong core again. "Bibu,

you don't know what you're saying. You're just confused—"

"I'm not confused. I know exactly what I'm saying."

"Love comes with—"

"Time, I know." I take a deep breath and meet Nick's gaze. "And sometimes it's love at first sight."

Nick's eyes flicker.

Ma glares at Mr. Basu, as if he's responsible for this whole debacle, but he shrugs.

"It's okay, Ma. Baba would approve."

The blood drains from Ma's face, and she leans back against Mr. Basu again. "Oh, Bibu—"

"Sometimes love comes in mysterious ways. Someone walks in front of you, smiles at you in the street."

Nick's watching me, as motionless as the air before a storm.

"What about Ravi?" Ma asks.

"I've already spoken to him," I say.

"He's come all the way from India!"

"He was coming here anyway, Ma. We would go through our whole lives just settling for each other, and that would not be right for either of us."

"Oh, Bibu. I can't believe you're doing this," Ma says. "What about the relatives? They will be so disappointed. And your Thakurma."

I think of Sita's mother, her harsh exterior, the way she softened and changed. "Thakurma is a strong woman, Ma, stronger than she lets on. And wiser. She will understand."

Ma presses a hand to her chest, pretends to have palpitations again.

Nick betrays no emotion. Maybe I hurt him beyond repair. Maybe he'll marry Liz, but I have to tell the truth, my truth, even if my heart breaks.

"Love!" Asha shouts. "So mysterious!"

I look at Nick, hope for a future, for something. But he gives no sign.

Ma sits in a chair and fans herself, Mr. Basu at her side.

I run to her and try to hug her, but she shrugs me off. "Ma, things will be better this way. I promise."

"Well, enough of all this hullabaloo," Asha says in a theatrical voice. "We have much work to do before my wedding!"

Thirty-eight

I visited Ravi at his apartment. He was not surprised, but maybe a little sad. And I saw a hint of another woman on the edge of his mind, a woman not yet in his consciousness.

He took my hands in his. "I somehow knew this would happen," he said. "I want to know you always. Our families share a past, a common culture."

"I'd like to talk to you about my father. I'd like to remember him the way he really was."

"We'll have tea, supper perhaps, and I'll tell you all I know." Ravi smiled a sad smile. My physical beauty drew him, and he had become smitten, but perhaps he would never come to love my true, deeper self.

Tonight, Ma and I are quiet at supper. Her eyes are red-rimmed. Her dreams of my perfect marriage have swirled away, but new dreams sprout. She's standing on the mountaintop with Mr. Basu, and now the fog clears and the image comes into sharp focus. Ma's in Darjeeling, bundled in linen and wool, a look of sheer joy in her eyes. Now I know—Mr. Basu's fierce love for Ma makes him handsome. He has always been loyal and good.

"I thought it was my marriage that would make you happy," I say. "I thought it was the success of the shop, but it wasn't, was it? I see you on the mountain with Mr. Basu. I think you should go there with him. Follow your dream."

"Oh, Bibu, I can't leave you."

"I can take care of the shop. It's what I'm meant to do—helping babies, girls, women find happiness, find their way. But you, Ma—"

"I always loved textiles," she says, clasping her hands in her lap. She gazes out the window again, always looking away. "I threw myself into that job to forget, Bibu. When Jamila visited the shop, I was devastated." Ma looks down at her hands.

"You don't have to talk about this—"

"I know your Thakurma told you about her, that you took Jamila's ring back to her. You see, we scuffled, and I yanked off the ring. It was loose on her anyway, had never been properly fitted. The ring brought such despair to my heart. I threw that ring. I didn't aim for the sink, but that's where the ring landed. I thought the sewer had long ago claimed it."

The air thickens and fills my chest, and grief pulls at my ribs. "Baba visited me in a dream. He tried to tell me that love comes in unexpected ways. Don't you see, you must pursue your happiness, Ma. It would make me happy to see you truly happy."

Ma's lips tremble. "I've dreamed of returning to Darjeeling with Sanjay—"

"And trekking the way you used to, I know, Ma."

"I couldn't leave you, Bibu."

"I'll be fine with Pooja, and I'll hire a couple of other helpers."

"I'll just go for a trip, nah? I can't leave for good when you are not yet married—"

"I'll be fine, Ma. I don't need to marry just now. I have to figure things out on my own."

Thirty-nine

Asha's wedding is resplendent, a bright jewel on a ship on the Puget Sound. Ma beams, all her costumes perfect. The caterer has prepared a feast of Indian food and sweets—biryani, curries, samosas, pakoras, lassis, gulab jamin, and jelabis. Champagne and expensive wine. Sitar and tabla players flew up from San Francisco. Emotions and dreams rise in bright stars above the ship, and the winter air grows warm with the power of happiness.

Ma and Mr. Basu and I step onto the deck. Mr. Basu looks smooth and polished in a Nehru suit. Ma's beautiful, bedecked in gold jewels and a golden sari, perfectly offsetting my bright blue sari with my enormous earrings. "You've outdone yourself, Ma," I say, beaming. Every outfit is a perfect creation.

"You are responsible for this, Lakshmi," Ma says. "It has always been your divine light that has helped our customers."

"Don't say that—you've worked so hard, Ma!"

"Look—they're filming!" Mr. Basu says.

The cameramen with their handheld cameras keep to the background, shooting from the sidelines.

Through the crowd, we spot Asha and her groom, Vijay. Her leg has healed, and although she still wears a bandage, she can stand on her own. Vijay's big hair puffs out on all sides, and his nose is more prominent than usual, but he's a smooth actor, charming everyone in his path.

The couple glides toward us and envelop us in hugs. Vijay looks handsome in his formal, off-white, gold-threaded kurta pajama, Asha a vision in the brilliant red sari. She's daring in gold jewels and a short choli revealing her belly button—but she's on the edge of fashion.

"You've done such a marvelous job, Mrs. Sen!" Asha beams with pride. "And Lakshmi—you look incredibly beautiful—" Her voice breaks off as Nick appears. He's to die for in a manila kurta pajama threaded with silver. My stomach turns somersaults. He's transformed, a blond Adonis in the fabric of the gods. The tailored cotton works magic, outlining his muscles, his bulk, accentuating his height. Rainbow colors fill my bubbles, bouncing along the deck, sticking to kurtas and hanging from scarves. I'm mute, submerged in the ocean.

"You're beautiful," Nick says. "Mrs. Sen, you're gorgeous. You did a great job with the saris."

I hardly hear Ma's reply. Nick and I are looking at each other, so much unspoken between us.

"Dance?" he asks.

It's a slow song, and he's pulling me onto the dance floor. He puts an arm around my waist, and instant fire races up through me, and I'm lost, the sensation undiminished over time. Our feet move in perfect synchronicity, the other wedding guests falling away—

He looks down into my eyes. "It was brave of you to say all that in front of everyone at the shop."

"I feel free, and a bit—scared."

"Did you mean what you said?" he asks. "About love at first sight?"

I nod, hardly daring to breathe. "Nick, I wonder. Could we start over again?"

"I thought you were happy with your life."

"I will be. How is Liz?"

"I'm not seeing her anymore."

"You don't love her?"

"I don't lie, Lakshmi. I loved you the moment I saw you."

Warmth spreads through me. "I think I love you too, Nick. I think the bubbles were love."

"Bubbles?"

"My feelings show up in weird ways."

He laughs. "I like weird."

"Do you still want to see me again?" I ask. "Or have I damaged our relationship beyond repair?"

"Everything can be fixed," Nick says.

"Like pipes under sinks?"

He grins, sweeping me across the dance floor. I feel all eyes on us, as if we are the only couple on Earth. "So Lakshmi, what about your Bengali traditions? Families bonding with families?"

"I want to know more about your family, Nick. They're very warm people. I like them."

"And they liked you. But what about your mother?"

"She and Mr. Basu are leaving on a trip. I think she wants to be free of the shop, Nick. I'll run the store for a while. What about you?"

"I'm leaving the limousine business," he says, gazing into my eyes. "I've been looking for another business venture."

My throat goes dry. "What kind of venture?"

"Whatever falls into my path. Serendipity."

"Nick—"

"I've been learning Bengali. Did I tell you?"

"You? Bengali?"

"Maybe someday, I'll be able to talk to your mother in her native language."

Then he kisses me, so fast that I don't have time to think. This time he's not romantic and soft, but demanding, his lips firm, opening my mouth and taking. I'm lost, drowning in a vast sea of brilliant bubbles. He pulls me to him with a slight groan. "Oh, Lakshmi. Don't leave me again. Don't go off meeting other men—"

"I won't, Nick. I promise."

"I have to show you something." He pulls a small shiny object from his pocket and slips it on my finger. "Jamila sent this to me. She said she had no use for it now—I had the engraving changed."

"Oh, Nick." It's the ring! Inside are my initials and the Bengali words, *I love you.*

"*Thanda lege jabey,*" Nick says, holding me close. "Let me keep you warm."

Forty

Nick and I own the shop together now. We have two new clerks and a steady stream of business. Ma and Mr. Basu send photos from Darjeeling. They're standing on a mountain trail strewn with pine needles, their cheeks pink from the cold, steam rising from their mouths. They're laughing into the camera. Ma's happiness emanates from her letters in bursts of tiny violets.

Mitra's father attended her dance performance, and when he saw her spinning in that yellow costume, he broke down and cried. After the dance, he hugged her for a long time, and he and Mitra went home and talked late into the night. That was a few weeks ago. He passed away quietly, in his sleep, last weekend. Mitra is flying to India to spread his ashes in the sacred Ganga River.

It's springtime, a rare clear Saturday after a rain, when the tulips and daffodils bloom, cherry blossoms open in bursts of pink cotton, and the chickadees alight in the Douglas fir trees.

Nick is busy building a high shelf to stock a new shipment of silk saris. He's wearing jeans and a white kurta that accentuates the muscles in his shoulders. A succession of giggling teenage girls has been marching through all morning to see the gorgeous new co-owner, the American man who fixed the ceiling, installed a new front door and a new dressing room, and sells—saris! When he winks at the girls, they melt.

In the afternoon, a familiar woman walks in wearing a floral print dress and a white sweater, her face serene, her black hair in a braid down her back. She walks straight toward me. I recognize her eyes that smile. "Hello, Lakshmi."

"Rina!" I say, and nearly drop my coffee cup. "You look different. I mean, happy."

"The sari you gave me. It worked. The pallu stayed over my head, like magic. The sari didn't fall off. I looked gorgeous in it. My husband wanted me to wear it all the time."

"I'm so glad. How is your mother-in-law?" Gone back to India, I expect, or Rina would not be showing so much leg!

"She's still with us, but she has relaxed her rules. I took your advice and spoke to her about it." Rina looks at Nick on the ladder and lowers her voice. "I heard about your new business partner. Your husband, nah? Word is getting around. Some of my younger sister's friends are coming in just to get a glimpse of him."

"I noticed a few more girls than usual," I say. "Good for business."

"You're a very lucky woman," Rina whispers to me. "I've heard he is a wonderful man, kind and considerate, and—"

"Who's been telling you all this?"

"Pooja told me he drove her to her wedding rehearsal and then took you to a romantic lookout! Where is Pooja, anyway?"

"She's finishing her last year full-time at the university, and then she's going to San Francisco for medical school," I say. "Dipak is going with her. I'll miss her."

"And your mother. She's off in India, I hear."

"And enjoying herself tremendously."

Mrs. Dasgupta rushes in then, waving the *Seattle Post*. "Oh, Shiva! I see this article in the newspaper about this Nick selling saris with Lakshmi. Can you imagine? Oh, Shiva. I've come to see how this Nick plans to make the shop much better for Pia Dasgupta." She stops and stares up at Nick.

He glances over his shoulder, and my face heats. He steps down the ladder and takes Mrs. Dasgupta's hand. "Pleased to see you again, Mrs. Dasgupta. You're looking more beautiful than ever."

Mrs. Dasgupta pats the white bun on the back of her

head. "The Light & Lovely cream has been working." She elbows me. "And what about the two of you, practicing the Kamasutram, no doubt?"

My ears are on fire.

"You bet," Nick says and winks at her. "And I hope you are getting on well with your new husband?"

Mrs. Dasgupta's lashes flutter. "The Kamasutram is not at all what you expect, nah? We have tried all sixty-four—"

"Mrs. Dasgupta!" I cut in. "We have a new shipment of shawls just for you."

"Ah yes, and your husband will show me?"

"My pleasure." Nick helps her find a shawl, chatting with her the whole time, and then Chelsea comes in with Lillian, who is holding Jeremy's hand. He's carrying a swatch of sky-blue sari, holding the soft fabric against his face.

"We wanted to come and congratulate you," Lillian says and hands me a sophisticated drawing of the blue sky expanding above a boy and his mother. They're not touching each other, but they're both smiling. Jeremy doesn't talk much, but he is an unusually bright and talented child.

I hug Lillian and Chelsea. "Thank you. I'll cherish this forever."

Jeremy looks up at me, his cheeks pink. "Sky-room," he says, and grins.

What more could I ask for?

Nisha calls later that week. She left her high-powered

banking job to pursue the dream of her heart. She wore the imperial violet sari to a job interview, and she got a position as a counselor at a local university. She's attracted to one of the other counselors, but she's taking it slow.

I will take life as it comes too. I find solace in knowing that I'm true to myself, and one day, I receive a letter from Thakurma.

> *Dearest Lakshmi,*
>
> *Everyone thought I was on my last legs, but Dr. Prasad says I've mysteriously improved and may have many good years ahead of me. Funny the way life works out, nah? I was of course disappointed that you chose not to marry Ravi Ganguli, but then, we make new discoveries every day, don't we? Like finding rings in sinks.*
>
> *I do hope to make a trip abroad soon, now that I am stronger.*
>
> *With love,*
> *Thakurma*

Life is full of surprises, Baba, isn't it?

I'm happy here with Nick. We're saving the world, one sari at a time.

Acknowledgments

Deepest thanks to my editor, Maggie Crawford, for her insight, expertise, and guidance. Thanks to Mara Sorkin for all her hard work. I'm always grateful to my agent, Winifred Golden, for her advice, support, and uplifting sense of humor.

My deep gratitude to critiquers who patiently read the manuscript—or pieces of it—in various incarnations: Kate Breslin, Michael Donnelly, Lois Faye Dyer, Rose Marie Harris, Dee Marie, Skip Morris, Penny Percenti, Susan Plunkett, Sheila Rabe, Krysteen Seelen, Suzanne Selfors, Elsa Watson, and Susan Wiggs. Titles are always difficult to dream up, and Susan Wiggs is a genius. Thanks for *Invisible Lives*.

ACKNOWLEDGMENTS

I'm grateful to my cousin, Tanya Mukerjee, for her wisdom regarding Indian marriage customs, and my cousin Sayantoni (Shy) Palchoudhuri, for information about Bengali saris, and for the wonderful phrase *Thanda lege jabey*. Many thanks to my parents, siblings, and to Randy, Daniela, and as always, my husband, Joseph. I'm indebted to my supportive colleagues at Milliman, Inc., and to my wonderful readers. Thanks for your letters!

Thank you to Natasha Jaksich, excellent editor, journalist, and friend, and Anju Naidu, owner of Maharanees Sari Shop in Kent, Washington, for letting me interview her about what it's like to run a sari shop, and for the lovely sari catalog.

For additional information, I consulted *The Sari: Styles-Patterns-History-Techniques* by Linda Lynton (Harry N. Abrams, Inc., New York, 1995) and *The Sari* by Mukulika Banerjee and Daniel Miller (Berg Publishers, New York, 2003).

Reading Group Guide

1. Works of magic realism mingle realistic portrayals of events and characters with elements of fantasy and myth. What role does magic realism play in this novel? How does Lakshmi's relationship with her namesake, the Hindu goddess Lakshmi, affect her life?

2. Lakshmi lives under the weight of her mother's "old-fashioned longings" for her to find a suitable Indian husband, produce several male children, and become financially successful. How do these expectations differ from those of mothers in other cultures? What specific cultural values do Lakshmi and her mother share?

3. Do you express your culture and personality in the way you dress? What role does clothing play in this story and in Lakshmi's ability to see the hidden longings in others?

4. Lakshmi thinks, "I'm helping women, one sari at a time." How do saris serve as catalysts for change for different characters?

5. Why does Lakshmi hide her beauty? Would you do the same thing if you were in Lakshmi's position?

6. When Lakshmi first meets Nick, she unexpectedly loses her sixth sense. Why do you think this happens? Is Lakshmi still able to help others without her special powers?

7. Lakshmi understands "the power of pride—and fear—that can make us turn away from what we want the most." She sees this in her clients and in her friend Mitra who cannot make amends with her dying father. Why does she feel compelled to help people reveal their hidden longings?

8. Lakshmi finds Nick and Ravi attractive in different ways. How does each man appeal to her?

9. When Lakshmi discovers her mother's secret, why does she feel so disconcerted by her mother's happiness?

10. What role does Jamila Tarun's wedding ring play in the story? How does it serve to help Lakshmi gain a deeper understanding of her parents and the choices they made?

11. Lakshmi's father visits her in a dream, and says, "There are things in life that happen by accident. Someone walks in front of you, smiles at you in the street. Serendipity." What is her father's message?

12. Do you believe that love grows over time or do you believe in love at first sight?

13. Do you have an invisible life? And if so, how much of it do you share with your family and friends?

Enhance Your Book Club:

1. Visit http://hinduism.about.com/od/artculture/ss/wearasari.htm for an illustrated step-by-step guide that teaches you how to wear a sari.

2. Visit the online sari shop, Sari Safari, http://www.sarisafari.com/, for a virtual textile tour through the tremendous range and variety of weaving, dyeing and embellishing traditions of the Indian sari.

3. For more interesting information about saris, read the book *The Sari* by Mukulika Banerjee and Daniel Miller (Berg Publishers, 2004).